God Bless the Trappers 2

Lock Down Publications and Ca$h
Presents

God Bless the Trappers 2

A Novel by *Tranay Adams*

Lock Down Publications
P.O. Box 870494
Mesquite, Tx 75187

Visit our website @
www.lockdownpublications.com

Copyright God Bless the Trappers 2017

Lock Down Publications
Like our page on Facebook: Lock Down Publications @
www.facebook.com/lockdownpublications.ldp
Cover design and layout by: **Dynasty Cover Me**
Book interior design by: **Shawn Walker**

Stay Connected with Us!

Text **LOCKDOWN** to 22828 to stay up-to-date with new releases, sneak peaks, contests and more…
Thank you.

Submission Guideline.

Submit the first three chapters of your completed manuscript to ldpsubmissions@gmail.com, subject line: Your book's title. The manuscript must be in a .doc file and sent as an attachment. Document should be in Times New Roman, double spaced and in size 12 font. Also, provide your synopsis and full contact information. If sending multiple submissions, they must each be in a separate email.

Have a story but no way to send it electronically? You can still submit to LDP/Ca$h Presents. Send in the first three chapters, written or typed, of your completed manuscript to:

LDP: Submissions Dept
Po Box 870494
Mesquite, Tx 75187

DO NOT send original manuscript. Must be a duplicate.

Provide your synopsis and a cover letter containing your full contact information.

Thanks for considering LDP and Ca$h Presents.

CHAPTER ONE

The large, thick, iron double doors opened outward with a loud squeal, and then Drennen came strolling out casually, taking a gander at his surroundings. He had a haircut so fresh that he still had hair inside of his ears. He wore his signature glasses and crucifix, along with a button-down shirt. His shirt was tucked into his slacks, which had a snakeskin leather belt that held them up on his waist. His pants were starched to a crisp, lying over some black leather shoes. His shoes were polished to a shine so fine that he could see his smiling face in them. The nigga looked like a corporate thug in his attire, especially with the gold Rolex watch adorning his wrist.

Drennen hoisted his sack over his shoulder and placed a jeweled hand over his brows, peering up at the beaming hot sun. He narrowed his eyelids and a smile stretched across his lips. Homie was happy to have his freedom. It had been a while since he'd been out in the world, and he planned to take full advantage of it. After taking a deep breath, the smile stretched further across his face. Although the air had smelled something awful, he welcomed it into his lungs. Having been incarcerated, he realized that it was the smaller things in life that mattered.

Drennen was about to begin his journey back to Los Angeles, when something far off in the distance grabbed his attention. Sitting his sack of belongings down on the ground, he removed his glasses and fogged its lenses with his breath. Whipping out a handkerchief, he flapped it out and used it to clean his glasses. He slid them back on his face, adjusted them, and narrowed his eyelids. Looking ahead, he spotted a red stretch Hummer on 28-inch chrome rims that was driving in his direction. He massaged his goatee, wondering who it was on board the sexy machine, but no one came across his mental. Drennen hoisted his sack over his shoulder and began his trek, when the humongous vehicle came to a halt before him, freezing him in his tracks. The Hummer was still and quiet. Instinctively, Drennen went for his waistline, but then he remembered he'd just been released from prison and he wasn't strapped.

Having realized this, he dropped his hand to his side and waited to see what was going to happen next. There was a prolonged silence, and then the back door opened and two bikini clad women slid out. One was bronze and the other was caramel, but they both were startlingly attractive. The moment that nigga Drennen saw them, he felt his dick nudge at his zipper. The caramel girl smiled and waved at him, batting her long eyelashes flirtatiously. While she was doing this, her counterpart ducked off inside of the vehicle and pulled out a sign, holding it to her chest. Drennen took a good look and saw that the sign had his government scrolled across it. Seeing this, he went on to approach the ladies. They ducked off inside and waited for him to climb in behind them. He did.

The bronze beauty broke out the champagne flutes and began pouring up the glasses. While she was doing this, caramel took the liberty to roll up a bleezy of that Loud. Having licked the blunt closed, she swept the golden flame of the lighter back and forth beneath it to seal it shut. She took a couple of puffs from the end of it and passed it to Drennen, who indulged in it as well. Before he knew it, the bronze girl was passing him one of the flutes. They all toasted to his freedom and bomb ass sex.

Drennen threw back what was left in his flute and set it aside. One of the girls gave him a black wooden box with golden locks on it. He took the time to pop the locks. Once he opened the lid, he found two golden envelopes, one of which was fatter than the other, and a Ghost Gun. A Ghost Gun was a firearm completely untraceable. It was expensive too, ranging anywhere from $5,000 to $10,000. Switching hands with the blunt, the first thing Drennen opened was the fat golden envelope. Once he had thumbed through all the bluish-green Benjamin Franklins inside, he closed it back up and sat it back inside of the box. Next, he opened the other golden envelope and pulled out the letter, which he unfolded and read. His eyes moved from side to side, as he fed his mind the information on the letter.

Drennen folded the letter back up and took the lighter from caramel. He set the end of the letter on fire and watched it curl up and turn black, as the flame ate away at it. He stared at the burning piece of paper with a serious, concentrated look in his eye. Next, he held down the button that operated the back window, descending it. The limo was speeding, so he could hear the noise of other speeding vehicles blowing past. Tossing the burning letter out of the window, he rolled it back up and went back to smoking. Drennen picked The Ghost Gun up from out of the box, checking its magazine and its sighting. Satisfied with the craftsmanship of the lethal weapon, he placed it back inside of its placement and shut the box. He sat the box beside him and, when he looked up, his hooded eyes saw the bronze girl was tearing open the golden foil of a Magnum condom and the caramel one was swiftly unbuckling his slacks. It wasn't long before his hardness was being pulled from its confinement, and the latex was being rolled down his shaft. The bronze girl slipped off her bikini bottom and squatted over his erection.

Taking it by its shaft, she guided it inside of her warmth, hissing like a snake as it filled her up. Once she'd found her rhythm, she went ham on the dick while her homegirl sucked on the ex-con's nut sack. Drennen threw his head back and his eyelids fluttered like a butterfly's wings, enjoying his homecoming gifts. His ears were flooded with the sensual moans of the women, the suction noise from his sack being sucked, and the noisy leather seat of the limo as he was being rode. Continuing to ride her fuck-buddy, the bronze girl took the blunt that was pinched between his fingers and took drags. She polluted the air with smoke as she worked up a sweat.

Drennen laid back, looking through narrowed eyelids with a smirk plastered on his lips. He was in heaven now. Omar broke him off with a nice chunk of change, set him up in a fully furnished apartment, gotten him clothes, shoes, and even a gun. All he had to do was take care of whatever business that his homeboy had for him and this nigga was financially straight. For now, he would enjoy himself because once he went to see his people and got his personal business in order, he was going to take care of the business that was assigned to him.

That night

Drennen had been having what he'd deemed the greatest night of his life. The girls that showed up in the stretch Hummer to get him from prison fucked and sucked the soul out of his ass. Them hoes had his head fucked up, performing sexual acts on him that he didn't even know existed. Their skill and knowledge on how to please the opposite sex reminded him of how long he'd been gone. It was okay though. He was going to take what he learned from them that night and use it on the next broads he laid the pipe to.

As of now, Drennen was trekking his way back from towards the double electric doors of CVS. He had run out of condoms and liquor, and the ladies were still good to go; they just needed a little incentive to keep the party going. Since he'd have the broads on deck until tomorrow morning, he figured he may as well take advantage of the situation. Not only did he purchase the condoms and alcoholic beverages of the ladies' choice, but he also grabbed a pack of Zig Zags for the weed he'd procured on his way over to the hotel.

Drennen crossed the threshold out of CVS and met the night's cool air. Flipping up the collar of his suit's jacket and tucking his chin, he gritted his teeth. Narrowing his eyelids, he shook a little, as he was trying to keep warm. Standing where he was, he allowed his neck to crane as he was looking for the stretch Hummer that he had until tomorrow evening.

A line creased his forehead. The supermarket's parking lot was scarcely occupied, which would make it easier for him to spot the chauffer driven Hummer, but it wasn't anywhere in sight.

"Where the fuck is this nigga, man? It's cold as a bitch out here." Drennen pulled out the cellular he'd purchased earlier that day and dialed up the chauffer. The phone rang and rang, but no one ever picked up. He tried again but, still, no one answered. Pissed off, he disconnected the call, just as the voicemail picked up and stashed the cellphone back inside of his pocket. He glanced at his Rolex and took another look around, taking a deep breath. Afterwards, he made his way through the parking lot, liquor bottles clinking inside of the brown paper bag he was toting.

Drennen was making his way down the block when he saw something stirring within the shadows out the corner of his eye. Quickly, he whipped his head around and narrowed his eyelids; he was hoping to see what he seen from his peripheral. At that moment, as if by magic, several individuals appeared clutching lethal weapons. They all wore ski masks over their faces. Instantly, Drennen's heart thudded inside of his chest and his adrenaline surged through his veins, raising his blood pressure. His eyebrows lowered and wrinkles formed at the beginning of his nose. His head snapped around in all directions as he switched hands with the brown paper bag, alarm wailed inside of his head. *Danger! Danger! Run! Run! Run!* He ignored it though. That would be the day that old Drennen ran from a fight; he was far from pussy.

Before Drennen knew it, a total of six men had surrounded him, coming at him from all angles. He was trapped in the ring of them. Seeing this, he cautiously sat his brown paper bag down on the sidewalk. Keeping a close eye on the visible threats, he slowly loosened his tie from around his neck and removed his suit's jacket. He then threw his suit's jacket high up into the air towards a tree. It landed perfectly on the end of one of the tree's branches, hanging itself there.

This situation was life or death, which was nothing new to Drennen. Hell, he'd faced situations like this back in prison. For him, this was just another day at the office. His head whipped around in every direction; his suspecting eyes took in the evil glares of the men itching to make him a statistic. The first had a katana, the second a switch blade, the third a Bo staff, the forth nun chucks, the fifth a chain and the last one, a machete. They were watching him closely and he was watching them, waiting for them to make the first move.

"Aaaah!" one of the men hollered out, charging forth with his Bo staff. "Ugh!"

Drennen kicked him in his chest and sent his ass flying back from where he came, staff going up in the air. He hit the ground hard, lying flat out and moaning in pain. A moment later, his staff fell to the ground on its bottom and landed on its side, rolling a little.

Bwrap! Bop! Crack!

Drennen's fists and feet came lightning fast. The attack he launched against his challengers brought them looks of excruciation, and this etched a sinister smile across his face. The drama made his dick hard; the mothafucka lived for it.

Ping! Ting! Clink! Ging!

The nun chucks, machete, switch blade, and katana hit the ground right after its owners did. Five of the six men were lying scattered on the ground with bruises and cuts on their faces. With them out of the fight, their comrade was left to fight Drennen alone.

The last man standing and Drennen circled one another, counter clockwise. They were locked into an intense stare down, examining one another while trying to figure out their next attack. The man with the chain held it at one end while he winded the other end with the padlock attached to it. Abruptly, Drennen stopped where he was and narrowed his eyelids at him. The nigga with the chain did the same but kept on whirling his weapon, making it spin around in a blur like a helicopter propeller. The old hitta cracked a smile and flicked his nose, licking his lips. He moved around like the skilled martial artist that he was. His challenger's face twisted with anger and he unleashed a war cry, swinging the chain in his enemy's direction. The padlock end of the chain came flying at Drennen's face. He jumped up in the air and kicked that shit, sending it flying back at his enemy. The man's face balled up in agony as he was cracked in his hairline by his own weapon. The assault split his wig open and a crimson river came spilling down his scalp, drenching his face. The impact from the attack sent his ass sailing backwards, legs going up in the air, showing the bottoms of his sneakers. He hit the surface and flipped over on his stomach, sliding across the ground. Grimacing, he attempted to get up, but his wound left him too weak to defend himself. He tried to push up off the ground and went slamming back down into it, busting his mouth. The defeated man took a last breath and blew debris up in the air.

Drennen stood where he was, taking a good look at all the niggaz whose asses he'd whooped. Seeing he had dispatched all the men that had come for his head, he threw his head back and took a deep breath, releasing tension from his body. His face and the back of his neck were beaded with sweat. Hearing clapping at his rear, he whipped around ready for more. His eyebrows were arched, his nose was scrunched up, his jaws were squared, and his fists were clenched. The hostility drained from his face once he saw someone approaching him from out of the shadows, steadily clapping their hands. The further the person advanced in his direction, the more of them was revealed, starting at his sneakers and ending at his face. Drennen acknowledged who it was standing before him, clapping their hands as if he had just finished watching an astonishing performance. Drennen let his arms drop at his sides, staring at the man that had approached him from out of the shadows. The old hitta's chest rose and fell as he breathed heavily, nostrils flaring, disturbing his nose hairs.

"What the fuck are you doing here?" Wonderment creased Drennen's forehead. He was completely taken off guard by the sudden appearance of his old friend.

"What do you think?" Omar asked.

A confused look spread across Drennen's face and he looked at all the men that he had laid out in the brawl. They were all lying on the ground moaning and bleeding, respective weapons lying not too far from them.

"Wait a minute, man, you mean to tell me that chu sent all of these mothafuckaz at me?" His hand swept around to all the men lying at his feet that he'd dispatched with ease. Although he was an older man, he was still quick on his feet. Locked up, he stayed in shape through jail workouts and ate as healthy as he could, under the conditions he was living under.

"Every last one of they sorry asses." Omar looked around at all the men that were lying on the ground moaning and groaning painfully. His forehead was wrinkled and his lips were twisted, as he shook his head. He hated he spent good money on the men. Although he knew that they couldn't possibly see his homeboy with the hands, he was hoping that the poor bastards would have at least given him a show.

"Five racks down the goddamn drain." He kicked one of the strewn men in their side, causing them to howl out in pain. He then spat on him and licked his lips. The nasty glob splattered against the man's forehead and dripped off his brow, landing on the sidewalk.

"Yo, Omar, fuck you sending niggaz for my head for?" Drennen scowled, curious as to what was going on because it really didn't make sense to him. Why in the hell would Omar send hittas to take him out, when he wanted him on his payroll?

"Loosen ya girdle, nigga. I had to make sure that you still had it." He took the time to light up a cigarette, cupping his hand around the flame and then blowing out a cloud of smoke. He then took the square from between his lips and tapped it, dumping grayish black ashes to the ground.

"Well." Drennen straightened out his shirt and brushed imaginary lent from off his button-down's sleeves. "Does the old man still got it or what?"

"Oh, you most definitely still got it. I'll be in touch." Omar polluted the air with more smoke and looked down the block, whistling. After he'd done this, he motioned over whoever he was looking up the street for. A moment later, an Excursion came to a screeching halt behind him, beside the curb. The enormous SUV's beautiful paint job gleamed underneath the illumination of the light posts lining the street. The front passenger window was down, so Candy could be seen behind the wheel, blowing huge bubbles out of her gum.

Once the bubble popped, she sucked the gum back into her mouth and started back chewing, motioning for her man to hop into the truck, saying, "Come on, daddy!"

"Welcome home, my nigga." Omar headed toward his Excursion. Throwing open the passenger door, he climbed into the front seat and slammed the door shut behind him. He took a pull from his cigarette and tilted his head back, blowing smoke up into the air. He then signaled for Candy to drive ahead and she obliged him, taking off into the night. She drove ahead until the red brake lights of the truck disappeared into the darkness.

Once Omar had disappeared, Drennen looked up the block at the enormous SUV for a minute. He then picked up his brown paper bag and walked off, heading back toward his motel room. He bopped from left to right, acting as if he didn't have a care in the world.

CHAPTER TWO

"Damn, girl, this shit feels good than a mothafucka," Kreon said, eyelids shut. He was lying on his stomach in bed; Odette straddled him. Her glistening hands were at work, massaging hot baby oil into his flesh. The way he was moaning and licking his lips, anyone listening would think that he was getting the blow job of his life. "Ssssssss, shit, Mocha, you went to school for this shit or somethin'?"

She chuckled and said, "Nah, I've had plenty massages though. I'm just applying what little I know to what I'm doing here."

"Well, you doin' one hell of a job, slim."

"Thanks, handsome." She smiled halfheartedly, continuing to work her magic on his meaty back.

"Mmmmmmm." A smirk stretched across Kreon's lips and he turned his head upon his chin, facing the black tint of the 55-inch flat-screen tv. He peeled his eyelids open and saw the pitiful expression across Odette's face, as she massaged his back. The skin on his forehead bunched together, as he wondered what the matter was with her.

"Sup, Hersh?"

She looked up at his reflection on the television and weakly smiled, shaking her head and saying, "Nothing." With that said, she went back to massaging his back.

"Nuh unh, we not finna start that shit." He tapped her leg and she climbed off him, allowing him to roll over on his back. She crawled over to him and laid her head against his chest, playing with his chest hairs as her moist eyes stared up at his. While she was doing this, he was rubbing his hand up and down her back. "What's up, baby? Talk to yo' nigga, let 'em know what's goin' on?"

Odette took a deep breath before she went on to tell him what was on her mind. "Your mother doesn't like me."

"What?" He frowned and sat up. "What makes you think that?"

16

"The first time we met." She went on to tell him about her and his mother's first encounter.

"Are you serious?" He frowned further.

"Yeah." She nodded fast, tears falling unevenly down her cheeks. He took the time to wipe them away with his finger and thumb.

"Come on, we going holla at mom's." He sat up on the couch bed and slipped on his clothes. She got dressed too, sliding her small feet into her black Air Force Ones last. Once he'd gotten fully clothed, he took his lady by the hand and led her to his mother's bedroom. Standing before it, he could hear the television from the other side; his mother was watching *16 and Pregnant.*

"That tv loud as a mothafucka on the other side of this door," Kreon said to no one in particular.

"Hold on, girl?" Kreon overheard his mother say to whoever she was on the cordless telephone with. "Who is it?" she called out loud enough for her son to hear through the door.

"The nigga you pushed outta yo' pussy," he responded back to his mother.

"Babe," Odette scowled and nudged him. "Don't talk like that to her; she's your mother."

Kreon looked at her and shrugged, before turning his attention back to the door.

"Watch cho mouth, and what do you want?" his mother asked.

"I needa holla at chu, old lady."

"About what?"

Kreon didn't even bother answering; he turned the knob and pushed opened the door. He found his mother snuggled under the cover with the cordless cradled to her ear. The blue illumination from a 40" flat-screen tv flickered on her person, as she talked on the phone and took the occasional pull from her Newport, polluting the air with smoke.

"Ma, I needa talk to you for a minute," Kreon told the woman that had given him life.

"The way you looking, it must be pretty goddamn serious."

"I'd say it was."

"Girl, lemme call you back. Nah, everything is alright. My son just wants to have a word with me. Oh, alright." She disconnected the call and sat the cordless on the nightstand, continuing to indulge in her cigarette.

"Ma," he began, hands together while shutting his eyelids briefly. "I don't need you checkin' every female that I bring through here. I'm not tryna wife up every skirt that chu see me with. I'ma grown ass man, I can handle myself. You gotta stop treatin' me like I'm some poor, defenseless goddamn kid!"

Odette looked from her man to Ella. She was staring at him and taking tokes from her cancer stick, like she didn't have a care in the world. She could feel the tension in the air with how heated Kreon was growing in his conversation with her. Since she'd known him, she knew how explosive his anger could be and she was fearful that he may end up putting his hands on his mother.

"Baby, you think you could bring your voice down just a-"

"Not now, O." He whipped his scowling face around to her, giving her a look that said *your ass had better be quiet or else.* He then turned back around to finish addressing his mother. "Back to what I was sayin', you owe O an apology."

"For what?" Ella sat up in bed and tapped her square, dumping ashes into the ashtray beside the bed on the nightstand.

"For threatenin' to harm her if she breaks my heart."

Ella glanced at Odette and then back to her son, eyebrows arching. "I wasn't just talking outta my ass, I meant what I said. If she hurts you, then I'm gonna-"

"O isn't going to break my heart, ma. 'Cause I don't have one to break. There ain't shit here." He smacked his hand up against the left side of his chest, clapping the fabric of his shirt against his peck.

"Baby, you-"

"Apologize." He gave her a stern look and his nostrils flared.

"But-"

"Now!" he snapped, startling her and causing her to shut her eyelids for a moment.

Swallowing the ball of hurt that had formed in her throat from her son talking to her the way that he was, Ella went on to peel her eyelids back open and apologize to Odette. "I'm sorry." She sniffled and her eyes twinkling.

"O, do you accept my momma's apology?" he asked, eyes lingering on his mother.

Holding on to Kreon's arm and looking his mother in the eyes, she said, "Yes."

"Okay, good." He went on to address his mother. "Momma, here's somethin' you needa understand. I'm your goddamn son; I'm not your man! So please, please, pleeease, stop actin' like I am! If you tired of bein' single, then find yo' self a man, 'cause I can't be it. I'm someone else's man, alright?" He stared her dead in her eyes.

She was glassy eyed. Not saying a word, she continued sucking on the end of her Newport, creating smoke clouds. His words had hurt her, but she wasn't about to let him see that they did. Ella didn't need to respond; the look on her face told him that she'd heard him loud and clear.

"Babe, come on." Odette tugged on his arm. She felt bad for bringing her concerns to Kreon now. She didn't expect him to wild out on his mother like that.

Kreon was standing there, staring at his mother while her eyes were focused on the tv, acting as if he wasn't even there. Her eyes had pooled with tears and she knew that, if she dared to blink, tears would slide down her cheeks. "Come on." She tugged his arm again. He lingered in the bedroom for a time longer, staring at his mother before walking off with his chick. As soon as he shut the door behind him, tears came running down her mother's eyes. She sniffled and the tears continued to flow.

***

Kreon came out of the apartment holding Odette's hand. He froze where he was when he saw Po and his homeboys loitering on the staircase, getting drunk and high as usual. That chicken head ass bitch Tranisha was out there too.

Seeing the strained look on her man's face, Odette's face balled up. "Bae, what's wrong?" she questioned with concern. Looking from him to the niggaz politicking on the steps, she realized why he had frozen in his tracks. "Aye, we can just chill inside of the house until they leave?"

With that, his head snapped in her direction and he narrowed his eyelids threateningly. Her suggestion caused him to angle his head to the side and look at her like she lost her goddamn mind.

"I ain't locked up, so I'll be damned if a nigga dictates when and if I leave my mothafuckin' house; let's go." He squeezed her hand tighter and moved forth, feeling at ease being that he had that steel on his hip. Kreon must have said excuse me a dozen times as he came down the staircase, making his way through the bodies on the steps and nearly knocking over plastic cups and bottles of dark liquor. Kreon and Odette had just stepped down to the surface, when that nigga Po grabbed a handful of her ass and squeezed. Odette jumped and her eyes lit up. Furious, she whipped around and smacked flames out of Po's ass. The impact whipped his head around and he held his stinging cheek, which had a red imprint on it.

"Nigga, don't chu ever put cho mothafucking hands on me!" She wagged her finger in his face. Her eyebrows were arched and her lips were twisted.

"Bitch, you musta lost yo' mothafucking mind puttin' yo' hands on my man!" Tranisha and her man's homies all hopped up ready for the bullshit, but that nigga Kreon put an end to that shit real quick.

In a flash, Kreon whipped that steel off his hip and waved that mothafucka around at all of those that opposed them. His face was fixed with a scowl and his jaws were clenched, pulsating.

"Whoa! Whoa! Whoa! Back the fuck up!" Kreon roared, spittle flying from off his lips. His hateful eyes studied the cock suckas before him; most of them had their hands up and were mad dogging him. He didn't give a mad ass fuck though; if they made a move, then he was going to send a couple of them to Satan's house.

"You a dead man, homeboy," Po gritted.

Kreon whipped out his car keys and passed them to Odette, telling her to get the car and pull up in front of the apartment complex. She went off to do as he had commanded, while he stepped up into Po's face. Abruptly, he kicked him in the nuts and doubled him over, eyes tearing. Next, he whacked him upside the head and dropped him in the driveway. Hearing someone trying to run up on him, he whipped around and pointed his banger into their face. It was Tranisha. That shit froze her in place and she looked scared than a bitch, shivering and shit. Smiling sinisterly, Kreon blew her a kiss and slowly backed away until he was in the street, where Odette sat in his car waiting for him. Seeing him approaching, she hurriedly opened the door and he jumped inside. He pulled his leg inside and slammed the door afterwards, giving his boo the word to pull off. As soon as the word was given, she was speeding down the street.

When they got to the end of the block, Kreon looked her over and saw the tears misting in her eyes. Her bottom lip quivered, and he grasped her thigh affectionately.

"You all right, Mocha?" he asked, concerned.

She shut her eyelids briefly and nodded her head rapidly. "Yeah, I will be."

"Good." He glanced over his shoulder but didn't see Po and his boys on them. This put him at ease for the time being, but he still didn't allow himself to get too relaxed. He was from the hood, so he knew better than to let his guard down. The shit could get popping again when you thought that it had died down. And it was just like he thought.

"Babe, they coming," Odette panicked, seeing a vehicle speeding up behind them in the rearview mirror.

"What?" He frowned.

"That's them behind us. The olive-green Corsica," she whined, tears threatening to spill.

Kreon looked over his shoulder and, as sure as his ass was black, there was an olive-green Corsica speeding up behind them. "Shit, that is them." He turned back around and checked the chamber of his revolver; it was fully loaded. He smacked that thang shut and tightened his grip on it. "Alright, you see this next light coming up?" He nodded to the stop light ahead. It was yellow and about to turn red. Odette nodded her acknowledgment of the stop light coming up. "Smooth, they drivin' up pretty fast on the side of us. Once I tell you to, slam on the brakes and lean over into my lap as far as you can. When I get off, mash the pedal and I'ma steer us up outta here, you Griff me?"

She nodded yes, tears cascading down her face. "Okay." He glanced up in the rearview mirror and saw the pursuing vehicle speeding up alongside of them. "Now!" he barked the order and she slammed on the brakes, ducking down in her man's lap. The Corsica came to a stop beside them. A mad-dogging Kreon pointed his ratchet at the nigga sitting in the front passenger seat.

"This what chu mothafuckaz wanted?" Kreon scowled, applying pressure to the revolver's trigger. He was just about to do whoever was in that passenger seat greasy, when his menacing eyes met a mother and her teenage son. They both screamed and trembled all over, seeing the hefty fella with the revolver pointed at them. Quickly, Kreon stashed his burner and apologized to the mother and son. Afterwards, he gave Odette the go ahead to drive off, and she did just that.

"What happened?" Odette asked, wiping her eyes with her hand before placing it back on the steering wheel.

"It was some kid and his moms." Kreon shook his head, shamefully. "I almost banged out a motha and her son. Damn, these niggaz got me out here trippin' fa real." He tucked his revolver on his pudgy hip. He then looked over to Odette and said, "You alright, momma?"

Odette nodded her head rapidly and replied, "Yeah, yes. Where... where are we gonna go now?"

"How about yo' spot? Lil' man at cho sista's house, right?"

"Yeah, we can go to my house."

"Cool." He interlocked his fingers with hers and brought her hand to his lips, kissing her knuckles. She gave him a smile, but he could see through it. Little momma was shaken up, and he couldn't blame her. Some real shit had almost happened, and someone could have ended up dead. He had grown up in The Concrete Jungle and she had grown up in West Hartford, Connecticut, so that kind of shit was foreign to her. His life was the shit that she saw in hood movies, and she'd yet to grow accustomed to it.

CHAPTER THREE

Once Odette and Kreon finally made it to her house, she had him make himself at home. He sat on the bed and turned on the television. Once he found something worthy of watching, he sat the remote control down beside him in bed. While he was watching tv, she grabbed her items she'd need for her shower, as well as something comfortable to wear for the night.

"I'll be right back." Odette leaned forth smiling and kissed him on the lips. She pulled back to find him smiling at her. She smiled back as she caressed the side of his face affectionately.

"Where you goin'?" He frowned.

"To take a shower," she answered. She turned to walk away but he grabbed her wrist, prompting her to turn back around. A wondering expression came across her face.

"Really though, O?"

"What?" She looked at him with confusion.

"You ain't gone gimme a kiss?" he inquired.

"Bae, I just gave you a kiss."

"That puss' ass shit wasn't a kiss, that was a mothafuckin' peck. Stop playin' and give yo' nigga some lip."

Odette cracked a one-sided smile and leaned forth again, kissing him. They pulled back from one another, smiling.

"Now, that was a kiss."

"Boy, you a trip." She sauntered off.

Still smiling, Kreon watched Odette walk to the bathroom, her plentiful buttocks dancing along the way.

"Goddamn, Mocha," he said, just a little too loud.

She'd heard him when she'd just pulled the bathroom door open. She looked over her shoulders and said, "What's up?"

"Huh? Oh, nothin'." He shook his head and focused back on the television.

Men, Odette thought, chuckling and shutting the bathroom door behind her. He didn't have to say anything because she already knew that he was talking about her ass.

***

Odette placed her towel and undergarments on the bathroom sink. She then disrobed and turned the dials of the shower. The showerhead sprayed hot water and a fog quickly manifested, converting the bathroom into a homemade sauna. Having tested the water's temperature with her hand, she discovered it was too hot and adjusted it to her liking. Next, she looked into the medicine cabinets mirror, pulling her braids back into a ponytail and making it into a bun. Finishing, she took a good look at herself through her reflection, turning her head from side to side. Satisfied, she smiled and stepped herself into the tub, one foot at a time. Sliding the door shut, she grabbed a loofah and the Shea butter Suave body-wash. She sung as she began to lather herself with soap, placing the body-wash at the corner of the tub.

Odette would forever cherish the night that she'd met Kreon at The Bar Fly. Although they'd started things off pretty well, their relationship hit a little turbulence. Still, little momma realized that relationships were difficult and took a lot of hard work. She fell in love with Kreon so fast and unsuspectingly, but she didn't regret it. God had given her a sign that he was most definitely the man that she'd ask him for, and she sure as hell wasn't going to block her blessings. Kreon made her feel beautiful and special in every way. She felt so safe and loved in his arms. She wanted to be with him forever and ever, and she was sure that he felt the same.

If you mess with my man, I'ma be the one to break it to ya

Got my girls, got my man, so find your own and leave mine alone

Don't mess with my man, I'ma be the one to break it to ya

Here's a little advice for you, find your own man

Odette was the happiest that she'd ever been in life since she started dating Kreon. He was loving, caring, kind, gentle, and he treated her remarkably. Sure, he was a little rough around the edges, but she figured that there wasn't anything that the love of a good woman couldn't fix. Although he wouldn't tell her his hardships, she knew that he had issues and she was willing to work with him. Her man was a stubborn asshole at times, but she was going to tough it out with him. After all, no one was perfect. And if it meant that she had to go through Hell to eventually reach Heaven, then she was more than willing to go on the journey.

Odette wasn't a fool; she understood that no one was perfect. And every relationship had its ups and downs. If she didn't know anything about relationships, she knew that much. She could remember a time when her parents seemed to be so in love with one another. So much so that she thought that they would never break up. They seemed inseparable. That was until her father, who was a small-time dope peddler, bossed up. He went from small time hustler to top dawg, seemingly overnight. His elevation in the game brought him a lot of attention from the opposite sex, a hell of a lot of attention from the opposite sex.

Odette's father, Willie, was a drug dealer out of east Hartford, Connecticut that had shit on smash. Homeboy was a flashy, flamboyant type of nigga; the mothafucka had to be seen. He had a mean murder game and fiercely loyal soldiers at his disposal. Not only was he feared, he was respected as well. He and his family were hood royalty. Homie was the king, his wife was the queen, and Odette and her older sister, Shonda, were the princesses.

Willie had taken his family out of the hood and moved them out to Greenwich to a big ass mansion. They had a butler, a maid, a chef, and a ground's keeper to make sure the lawn was well manicured. Margret and the girls didn't have to lift a finger.

Now, on the outside looking in, things appeared to be sunshine and blossoming flowers but, in the inside, shit was in total disarray. See, Willie's neighborhood dope man status had every woman in C.T. on his dick, jocking dude crazy hard. He busted a number of broads down on the low but, eventually, his creeping caught up to him in the form of an STD. The nigga caught the drip. You know, gonorrhea? Well, he passed that shit on to the girls' mother, and she was pissed the fuck off. But, that wasn't nothing some flowers wrapped in one-hundred-dollar bills, jewelry, and a brand new 600 Benz couldn't fix.

Margret forgave her husband's infidelity, but she found herself having to deal with it on a constant basis because the dog ass nigga couldn't keep his dick in his pants.

Willie made a fool out of Margret with his hoeing around town. Every bitch she caught him with, she was going upside their head, either fighting in the streets or slicing their mothafucking asses up. Homegirl didn't play that shit. She figured that, the more she brought it to bitches, eventually word would get around town that old Willie was her man and that hoes would keep their distance. She was wrong though. The hoes kept coming and he kept on piping them down. Pretty soon, Margret said fuck it and turned a blind eye to it. That was, until she found out that Willie's old trifling ass was fucking her best friend, Arnez.

Willie D sat on the toilet with a cordless telephone pressed to his ear, speaking in a hushed tone and trying not to be heard. "Yeah, I'ma slide on through there in about." Willie glanced at his Presidential Rolex before continuing on. "Half an hour. Nah, nah, nah, I told her I'ma be out in the streets takin' care of some bitness, so we good." He listened to what his mistress was saying to him as he looked himself over in the medicine cabinet's mirror, checking out his fresh haircut and adjusting his leather belt. "Wear that red joint I bought chu a couple of weeks ago. Yeah, that one was real fly. Alright, how's my baby do-"

Boom! Boom! Boom!

The bathroom rattled from the banging that it was taking from the other side. The sudden noise startled Willie. He nearly jumped out of his skin, whipping around to the door.

"Open this mothafuckin' door, Willie! You low down dirty bastard!" Margret called out from the opposite side of the door, raging mad. Old Willie could feel the heat come from her. She was as hot as a fire cracker.

"Yo, I'ma call you back," Willie whispered into the cordless telephone.

"Nah, you ain't gotta call the bitch back!" his baby momma roared, breathing fire. This caused his brows to furrow and he looked at the cordless like it stunk, realizing that Margret had been listening to his entire conversation from the other house phone. He ended the call and, ba-boom, the bathroom door came flying open. Margret threw the other cordless telephone at his head with all her might. The shit looked like a spinning blur, it came so fast at him. He ducked it just in time and it slammed into the ball, breaking on the side upon impact.

When Willie came back up from ducking, he was mad as shit. The nigga'z eyes were glassy and red and his nostrils were flaring. Gritting his teeth, he came speed walking in Margret's direction. By the time she made to run, he'd grabbed her by her neck and shoved her up against the bathroom door, choking her with one hand. She gagged and her eyes quickly built up with tears. Opening his palm, he cocked his hand back to smack fire out of her ass, but he stopped, seeing his daughters at the corner of his eye. When he looked and saw them looking scared, he released his wife and she slid down to the floor gagging and coughing.

"See how you got me in here actin' all outta character in front of my babies? I can't put up with this shit no mo' Margret. I'm packin' my shit and I'm gettin' gone...

tonight," With that said, Willie packed a suitcase and grabbed his hat. Margret followed him through the house hurling insults at him and promising him that no good would come to him, seeing as how he was abandoning his family. His daughters were right behind her, crying and begging him to stay. Once they acknowledged that their pleading was falling on deaf ears, they dove to the floor and latched on to their old man's legs.

"Daddy, please don't leave us, please!" Odette cried her eyes out, holding onto her father's leg as he dragged her and her sister along.

Willie struggled to make his way down the steps, suitcase in hand.

"Daddy, no, don't go!" Shonda called out, tears sliding down her cheeks. She was holding on to her father's other leg. The weight of her and her sister caused him to move like he was wearing cement shoes.

"I gotta go, now! I gotta go, I love y'all. The both of y'all." Willie bent down and pried their fingers from off his limbs, kissing their foreheads as they sat on their knees while looking up at him. When he brought his head back up, he howled in pain and his face balled up. A rock collided with his forehead and knocked off his hat, blood running from the bloody opening into his eye. His eyebrows arched and he gritted his teeth, looking up at Margret. She stood on the front lawn, chest heaving up and down. Her face was soaked with tears and fear was in her pupils, another rock clutched at her hip.

"Oh, what, you gone hit me now? Huh?" Margret asked, figuring that if he came back and wailed on her some more that he still loved her but, if he left, it proved that he didn't give a shit about her. That's how fucked up her thinking was. The bitch was crazy as a shit-house rat.

"Nah." Willie pulled a handkerchief from his shirt's pocket and dabbed the blood from his eye, wiping some from his forehead as well. Once he was done, he stuffed the handkerchief inside of his pocket and snatched up his hat from off the ground, placing it back on top of his head and adjusting it to his liking. "I'ma do you one better and leave yo' crazy ass." Listening to his little princesses begging him to stay, Willie cupped each of their faces and kissed them on their forehead. He then proceeded towards his car with them and their mother following him.

"Where you going, Willie? You think you just gone leave us, huh?" Margret dropped the rock and darted out of the yard behind her daughters, en route towards their father.

Willie hopped in behind the wheel of his midnight-blue Mercedes Benz C-class and cranked it up, pulling off. Adjusting the rearview mirror with tears in his eyes, he looked through the back window, seeing the three women in his life. They were all chasing after his vehicle, running as hard and as fast as they could, tears streaming down their cheeks.

Margret and Shonda had begun to tire and slow down, eventually stopping. Margret held Shonda in her arms and they looked on at the brake lights of the Cadillac, red lights shining in the darkness. Odette was still chasing after her father's car, breathing huskily. Her lungs were on fire and her legs were hurting, as she ran in her sandals. Water pooled her eyes, spilling down her cheeks. The wind blew, ruffling her dress and disturbing her individual braids.

"Daddy, don't leave us, please! Don't leave us, we love you! Me and Shonda still love you..." Odette's words were cut short as she tripped and fell, foot coming out of her sandal. She hit the street hard, scraping her knee and the palm of her hand. Wincing, she looked to her palm, seeing small dots of blood appear from the shredded skin. Her hand burned like it was on fire, but she didn't care about that; she wanted her old man. Vision obscured by tears, she looked up at the brake lights of the Cadillac. Its red lights were growing smaller and smaller; eventually, they disappeared.

Unable to withstand the sight of his sobbing daughters, Willie turned the rearview mirror from out of his line of vision. He turned on the stereo to take his mind off what had occurred, losing himself in an old Bootsy Collin's song.

I'd rather be with you, yeah
Yeah, I'd rather be with you
I'd rather be with you, yeah
Yeah, I'd rather be with you

"Daddy... please don't go," Odette outstretched her hand before her eyes, like she could touch her father from her distance. Realizing that this was impossible, she dropped her arm and bowed her head. Big teardrops fell from her eyes as she sobbed, shoulders rocking back and forth. She looked over her shoulder feeling a hand grasp her shoulder, finding her sister standing over her. Her eyes were glassy, pink, and her cheeks were slicked wet, but she wasn't crying any more.

Shonda pulled her little sister to her feet and wrapped her tightly in her arms. Her hand swept up and down her back, soothing her. It felt good being in the embrace of someone that loved her, but that didn't stop the tears from falling.

"Daddy don't love us, Shon Shon; daddy don't love us no more," More tears slid down Odette's face.

"That's not true, don't say that, Missy. He still loves us; he'll be back... you just watch and see... he'll be back," Shonda assured her, holding back tears of her own.

"That nigga ain't comin' back." Hearing their mother's voice startled them and they turned around, finding her lighting up a cigarette. Margret's face was shiny from crying too, but she had this evil look on her face that couldn't be explained. Some people that encountered her swore up and down that she was the devil. No matter how much she smiled or how pleasant she was... that evil look never left her face. That shit was like a birthmark.

Margret sucked on the end of her cigarette and blew out smoke before continuing, "Yo' daddy is gone to play house with that bitch and her kids. He don't give a fuck about me or y'all asses." She took another pull from her cigarette and expelled smoke. "From now on, it's just the three of us. That's it, just us three."

Without the financial support of her husband, Margret was forced to move her and her kids back to West Hartford. They stayed out there with the girls' grandmother until she eventually graduated from the R.N. program (registered nurse program). From there, she started stacking her money and bought a nice, big house for her and the girls to live in. She bought the girls any and everything that they wanted to make up for their father not being in their lives as much as he used to. It was a nice gesture, but it didn't make up for his absence.

It wasn't long before Margret began to resent her girls because she couldn't keep a man. She believed it was because she was a woman with two little girls. And there weren't too many men that were dying to marry some chick and help her raise some other nigga'z kids. This was her rationale for niggaz fucking and ducking her afterwards. She believed that this was the reason why she could only get a man to sex her but no commit to her. With that in mind, she took it out on the girls. She abused them verbally and physically whenever she felt like it. Later, she'd apologize for it and buy them something that they wanted, thinking that it would make things better but it didn't. Without realizing it, she was setting her daughters up to expect this treatment from men when they grew up.

Willie made arrangements with Margret in regards to their children. He would get the girls every weekend and pay her child support once a month. The girls' father was consistently in their lives for a year straight. But, suddenly, the weekend visits and the child support payments stopped. They tried to call him and discovered that his number had been disconnected. When they went by his house, there was a 'For Sale' sign in the front yard. The girls were heartbroken and devastated about their father's abrupt disappearance from out of their lives. His abandonment of them left them hurt and very confused.

Margret ran into an old worker of Willie's and got his number from him. When the girls called, Arnez answered and told them that their father didn't want anything to do with them anymore. They didn't believe her, so she put him on the phone and he told them exactly what his new bitch had already relayed. The girls broke down screaming and crying, pleading with their father to not abandon them. In return, they heard the click of the receiver as the telephone was hung up on them.

Years later, they ran into their father at a McDonald's on Flatbush Avenue. He was sitting outside of the establishment on a crate, begging for spare change with a cup scarcely filled with coins. He was wearing an apple-jack, dingy t-shirt and an overcoat. His facial hair was as thick as wool and his face was discolored in certain areas and had blemishes. The man stunk something awful. He was on heroine really bad, too. The girls could tell this from his swollen feet and hands. The mothafucka's hands were the size of boxing gloves. The same kind of boxing gloves boxers wore to fight with.

Odette and Shonda didn't know it was their father at first. It wasn't until he lifted his head and they saw the birth mark below his eye that was the shape of Africa that they realized that it was him. They ignored the foul stench coming from him, hugging and kissing on him. They hit him with a barrage of questions, which he answered.

"Daddy, how come you said that you didn't love us and didn't want to talk to us anymore the last time we talked, huh? What did me and Shon Shon ever do to you? All we wanted you to do was be our father and love us," Odette asked, wiping the tears that slid down her cheek with her curled finger. Seeing her crying, Shonda gave her a sisterly hug and gave her a couple of Kleenexes from out of her purse.

Willie bowed his head while his daughter was talking to him. When he brought it back up, his eyes were glassy and his face was shiny from crying. "Girls, you gotta believe me. I didn't want to say what I said, but I was out here down bad off them drugs. I was fucked up. I'd pissed away every dime and asset I had getting high. I didn't have notta pot to piss in or a window to throw it out of." He sniffled and wiped his eyes with the back of his hand.

Seeing this, Shonda handed him a couple of Kleenexes. She rubbed his back soothingly as she and Odette listened to him finish his story. "Arnez promised me that she'd take care of me and buy me all the drugs that I want, just as long as I disown y'all and ya motha. I tried to fight it, but that monkey got a hold of me and it just wouldn't let go. I was cramping and throwin' up like a sick goddamn dog. It was a life or death situation, so I didn't have a choice. I agreed to her terms and conditions, in order to get what I need. That same day that y'all called, I'd made the deal. She was dangling a packet of some of the meanest dope in the streets, Headache. That's why I said what I said that day baby but, as God as my witness, I didn't mean it." He raised his huge right hand.

Odette and Shonda hugged their father and they all started crying. Once they had finished their tender moment, the girls asked him where was Arnez now? He told them that she'd tossed him aside for some young trap nigga that could take good care of her, like he'd once taken care of their mother. The girls shook their heads pitifully, feeling sorry for their father.

"Listen, dad, we're gonna get chu out of here. You can come stay with me. We'll see about getting you into a rehab program so that you can get clean and see about getting your life back on track. How does that sound?"

"Like music to my ears, but can you do me a favor?" he asked.

"Sup?" Shonda threw her head back like what's up.

"I'm starving like Marvin; could you and yo' sister please go inside this McDonald's and get me two Big Macs, medium fries and a vanilla shake? I'd sho' appreciate it." He rubbed his stomach.

"Don't worry, daddy, we'll hook you up. Come on, Missy." Shonda motioned for Odette to follow her inside of the popular establishment. She ordered them something to eat and then she placed her father's order. Once they came back outside, it was like her father had vanished up into thin air. Odette's bottom lip quivered and she cried, thinking that she'd never see her father again. It took for her sister to comfort her before she eventually calmed down.

Shonda bottled up her feelings and moved through life like she wasn't fazed, but that was bullshit. The girl was self-medicating with liquor and weed to get over the hurdles that were her troubles. Odette, on the other had, developed daddy issues growing up. Like most young women like her, she started dressing revealing and seeking the love and affection from men that she didn't get from her father. The men that held her attention only entertained her because she was young and had the body of a grown woman. You know? A great big old ass and tits. These niggaz were older, so they were way more seasoned when it came to the opposite sex. Plus, they had tongues as slick as Crisco oil; if they could finesse women their ages out of their panties, a teenage girl didn't stand a chance against the G that they were spitting.

For a couple of years, Odette was promiscuous. But then, she figured out that all men wanted from her was sex. She wanted more than that though. See, she wanted to be in a committed relationship with someone that actually loved and cared about her. She was looking for a man to build with and to hopefully someday make a family with. With that in mind, she stayed celibate until she was eventually introduced to

Carlos through a friend of hers. They hit it off and she discovered that he wanted the same things in life that she did. They decided to take things slow but, as time went on, they agreed to be together. They vowed not to have sex until they got married, and they didn't. Marquise was conceived on their honeymoon night and he made his debut ten months later at Hartford hospital, weighing in at seven pounds and nine ounces. They were one big happy family, until Carlos decided to start beating her ass and creeping on her.

The dials squeaked as Odette turned them, shutting the flow of hot water from the showerhead off. She slid open the shower door and grabbed her towel from off the sink. Having dried herself off, she wrapped the towel around her bosom and took care of her hygiene. Next, she got dressed in what she was going to wear that night and sprayed herself with perfume. Little momma looked herself over in the mirror and took a deep breath, smiling from ear to ear. Satisfied with her appearance, she left the bathroom, looking forward to alone time with her boo.

God Bless the Trappers 2

CHAPTER FOUR

When Odette came out of the bathroom, she was in a t-shirt and sweatpants. Seeing the outlining of her big breasts and that big old ass of hers in those sweatpants caused a tingling sensation to come to life in Kreon's loins. He wanted to jump her bones but reasoned that he had to keep himself in check. Chances were, she wouldn't be in the mood to start something, with what had happened and all.

Odette walked past him, ass cheeks jiggling along the way. His eyes followed her ample bottom, as she came around him and crawled into bed. He focused his attention back on the television, acting like he was really into the show on the screen. It wasn't until she poked him with her little foot that he turned around to her, eyebrow raised.

"Why don't chu kick off your shoes and crawl into bed with me? I'ma little shaken up about everything and I'd like you to hold me, please." She looked at him with teary eyes that begged for his loving embrace. He nodded yes, kicking off his shoes and removing his hoodie. Whipping out his blue steel .38 revolver from his hip, he placed it down on the nightstand and slid in bed under the sheets beside the lady that held his affection hostage. She snuggled up next to him and threw her leg over his, resting the side of her face against his chest. As she shut her eyelids, he rubbed her back soothingly. He then kissed her on top of the head. When he did this, she looked up into his eyes and saw the blue illumination of the television flickering on his face, as he did hers.

A moment of silence passed between them before she took the lead. Her plump lips mashed against his and they kissed hard and passionately, husky breaths between them. It wasn't long before Kreon was sliding off Odette's t-shirt and revealing her succulent breasts, and she was unbuckling his belt. They found themselves as naked as Adam & Eve in the Garden of Eden, making out with the tv's blue light flickering on them. Suddenly, Odette pulled away from him and looked into his eyes. She then looked down at her body, quickly pulling the sheets back over her. All of a sudden, she remembered what she looked like underneath her clothes. She thought that, if she felt like her body wasn't desirable, she could imagine what he thought.

"What's wrong, Lover?" He caressed the side of her face with a curled finger. She shook her head and swiped away the tear that ran down her cheek. Seeing this, he turned her to face him by her chin, his thumb pressed against it. "What's the matter, babe?" She shut her eyelids and tears jetted down her face. He looked to the sheets that she held against her and realized that she was insecure about her body. Instantly, he acknowledged that was the reason why she didn't get fully undressed back at the lake when they had sex.

"We don't have to do this if you don't want to," he told her, seeing that she was uncomfortable.

"No, it's not that... it's..." she trailed off and looked down, embarrassed.

Kreon stepped to Odette and tilted her chin with a curled finger so that she'd be eye to eye with him. "What's wrong, Lover?" He searched her eyes, finding confusion inside of them. His forehead indented with a line.

"Kre... Kreon, I really like you and I don't wanna turn you off."

"What?" he chuckled, like she was being silly. "Why would I be turned offa you? I'm very, very attracted to you, sweetheart." He rubbed her shoulders and smiled at her.

"I'm afraid that you will see something on my body that you don't like and you won't want me anymore..." Her voice cracked under her raw emotions and tears broke loose down her cheeks. She licked her lips and tasted the saltiness of them, her body trembling; she shamefully casted her eyes down at the surface.

"Awww, babe, there is absolutely nothing that could turn me offa you." He cupped her face with his hands. "I love any and everything there is about chu. To me, even your imperfections are perfect, 'cause they make you, you. 'Cause without them, you wouldn't be who you are, you wouldn't be my Hershey's Kiss; the woman that I'm madly in love with." She broke down, shuddering and sobbing hard. He kissed her on the top of her head and took her by her wrist, leading her towards the dresser. "Come on, baby." He faced her to the dresser's mirror and went to turn on the light in the room. Seeing where he was going, she tried to stop him, but it was already too late; the lights restored life inside of the bedroom.

"Shit, what're you doing? Turn the light back off," she urged him, using her arms to cover up what she believed was a flawed body.

"Nah, I want chu to see somethin'," he said, walking toward her in his birthday suit.

"See what?"

"See what I see whenever I look at chu." He stepped behind her, looking over her shoulder and into the mirror at their reflections. Until then, she hadn't noticed the washcloth in his hand. Gently, he wiped away her tears with it and stood behind her again, staring at them through the mirror. He marveled at her face and body, but how couldn't he? She'd stolen his heart. Something someone had never done, something he thought no one could ever do but, somehow, she had.

Grasping her wrists, he slowly removed her arms from around her form. She tried to resist them, but there was always something about his touch that weakened her. He was like her Achilles' tendon. Tears welled up in her eyes as she stared into the mirror, watching him watch her. She hated what she saw staring back at her. Her body was hideous, really hideous, she believed. She just knew in her mind she was disgusting, and he was thinking the same.

"It's ugly, so ugly," Hot tears flew down her face and her nostrils flared. She looked away, unable to bear the sight of her own body.

"Nuh unh, stop that shit now." He turned her chin around so that she would be staring back at the mirror. His face was a mask of seriousness. "There's nothing wrong with your body, Hershey. It's beautiful. Hands down the most beautiful body I have ever seen."

"Please," she sniffled. Her eyes were glassy and pink from crying. "You're just saying that to make me feel better. I mean, are you blind, man? Look at me, look at my reflection. I gotta nasty scar on my forehead from when my mother clocked me with an iron. Burn marks going up my arm from her burning me with a curling iron. An old gunshot wound on my chest, stretch marks on my stomach, and I'm missing a tooth on the side of my grill." She clenched her teeth and turned her head to the side, showing off two of her missing teeth. Her husband had knocked her teeth out of her head because she refused to have sex with him. That thought alone made her drop her head and break down. Her shoulders trembled, as big teardrops fell from her eyes. She covered her body back up, but Kreon took her hands down again, lifting her head up by her chin. Taking his washcloth, he dabbed her face dry again and tossed it aside.

"These scars that you're so ashamed of tell a story," he began, locking eyes with her in the mirror. "A story of a warrior princess, who has been in many battles in life; it was in those battles that she was triumphant, victorious. Life could not beat her; it did not break her 'cause she wouldn't allow it. You know why?"

"Why?" her voice cracked again, but she kept eye contact with him through their reflection. She sniffled and wiped her nose with a curled finger.

"Because she's a survivor, a testament that nothin' could keep a strong woman down. That her will to live was stronger than her notion to give up and die."

"Oh, really?"

"Yes," he spoke sternly. "You wear those scars on your body like a purple heart. You know who they give purple hearts to in the army?" She shook her head no. "Soldiers... for fightin' bravely in war, and that's what you've been doing Mocha, fighting a war. You should be proud of yourself. I know I, for one, admire you," he said with a hand to his chest.

"How come?" Her forehead wrinkled.

"You've been through a hell of a lot and you're still here, still standin' strong."

This caused her to smile and show off that perfect set of white teeth.

"Look at that smile." He grinned.

She smacked her hands over her face as she turned red from embarrassment. The way he looked at her always made her uncomfortable. Strangely, she liked it though; it made her feel like the prettiest girl in the world.

"Unh unh, you betta stop now; you know how I feel about that smile." He took her hands away from her face. He held her hands at her sides, as he continued to stare into those brown eyes of hers. "Look at my, baby. Man." He took a deep breath and shook his head.

"What?" she beamed, feeling better than she was before.

"It's something about that smile of yours that just... it just takes my breath away."

"Kre... Kreon."

"Yes, baby?"

"Do... do you really think I'm a pretty girl?"

"Naaah." He shook his head. She lowered her head, being in her feelings again. He lifted her head back up by her chin, so they'd be seeing one another eye to eye in the mirror. "I think you're a pretty woman." With that said, she smiled through her tears. He wiped them away with his fingers, and she turned to him.

"Kreon." She looked up at him, hands against his chest.

"Yes?" he asked, caressing the side of her face.

"I don't wanna fuck."

"It's cool, Boopity Boo Bop. We don't have…"

"I want chu to make love to me."

"Okay." He nodded.

"Oh, my God." She looked away and shook her head, shamefully.

"What's the matter?" he inquired, as he rubbed her back soothingly.

She looked back at him and said, "I'm 27-years-old and I've never been made love to."

"I've never had anybody I love make love to me, until now." He lifted her chin with a curled finger and kissed her hard, passionately. Her nipples puckered and her pussy grew with moisture. As they kissed, his hand slid down her torso over her stomach and found that hidden treasure of hers. She hissed as his fingertips traced the slit of her vagina, lifting both of her arms and gripping the back of his head. Odette shut her eyelids and tilted her head back moaning, biting down at the corner of her bottom lip. She felt her lover's middle finger pierce her southern lips, being coated by her moisture. He fucked her with his finger and her face contracted, drawing wrinkles towards the center of her face. She parted her thick thighs to allow him further into her temple, toes twiddling. She licked her lips and rotated her hips like she was riding his dick. Whining and rising to the tips of her pedicure toes, feeling herself about explode.

Suddenly, her eyelids stretched wide open and her mouth elongated, arching her back. Her entire form shivered, as she came all over his hand. He sucked her pussy's nectar from his fingers, as he stared her in the eyes. Afterwards, he grabbed her by her hand and led her over to the end of the bed. Here, he pushed her down up on it and scaled her small body like a building. Once he reached her head and came into eye contact with her, they both smiled and chuckled.

Then, at the same exact time, seriousness washed over their faces. Suddenly, he licked her up her neck and sucked on her throat, causing her to shut her eyelids and gasp. Next, using the tip of his tongue, he traced her jaw line until he came across her chin for the second time. It was here that he nibbled and then came back up, kissing her lips. Slowly, he slipped his tongue inside of her mouth. They shut their eyelids and their heads turned in opposite directions, as they kissed hard and passionately. Their heavy breathing and saliva sloshing around in their mouths filled the air.

Kreon moved down Odette's center, planting kisses as soft as rose petals until he met the middle of her full chocolate breasts. He took a breast into each of his palms, mashing them together and tracing her areolas with his wet tongue. Next, he flicked his tongue across both nipples of the breasts, causing them to grow rigid. He then latched his warm, wet mouth onto her titties, closing his eyelids and sucking on them like a starving newborn. This caused her eyelids to flutter and her to moan like a dead man walking. Kreon went back and forth between his lover's tits, giving them both the equal amount of attention that they deserved. Odette squirmed underneath her man's handling of her.

Having released her breasts, he picked up where he had left off, biting her sensually down her center until he met her navel. He stuck his tongue inside of it and French kissed it, turning his head to the side like he did with Odette. He pushed her legs back open and softly bit on her inner thighs, making his way towards that stiff flap of meat that sat nestled between her full pussy lips. He blew his hot breath on her clit and she twitched and groaned, eyes fluttering once again. Abruptly and, without warning, he flicked that flap of swollen meat between her vagina lips with his tongue. When he done this, she whined and pulled at the sheets on the bed, wrinkling them. Right after, he was sucking on her clit as if it was a piece of Butter Scotch candy. This drove her wild and she couldn't help but to call out.

"Baaaeeeee!" she called out in sexual bliss, forcing her head back further into the queen-sized mattress and arching her back up from off it.

She then grabbed him by his head and pressed his entire face inside of her coochie; he sucked that much harder. Her eyelids shot open and she wrapped her thick legs around his neck, locking him into place.

"Move yo' fucking hands, nigga!" Grabbing her wrists, Kreon pinned her arms down to the bed and continued to devour her treasure. Her form shook uncontrollably and she squirted in his face, pleasure written all over her face.

"Ooooooh, faaaaatha! Ahhhhh!" Odette's face scrunched up and she gritted, spraying the lower half of her significant other's face. He continued to devour her as her legs trembled, heart beating so fast that her chest thumped rapidly. She moaned lowly as he sucked and nibbled on her inner thigh. Her orgasm had her exhausted and, although his mouth was magical, she couldn't wait for him to come up off that dick. "Oh, bae… oh, bae, I can't take it no more. I need some… I need some dick."

Kreon pulled his head back and the lower half of his face was glistening. He wiped his mouth with the back of his fist and crawled into the bed. Grabbing her from underneath her hips, he dragged her to the end of the bed and took his meat into his hand. He slid his hand up and down his steel, causing the head of it to swell and then shrink. His dick was as hard as a brick now and oozing pre-cum from out of its head. Using his thumb, he rubbed the jizz into the tip of his grown man, before sliding it into her heavenly opening. Her eyes grew big and she gasped, feeling his girth fill her up to capacity. He held her legs far apart and started off slowly, moving in and out of her hot, gooey hole. She felt good, so good that he hissed and threw his head back, enjoying her tunnel of pleasure.

"Ahhhhh, shit, babe…" His eyelids flickered and he bit down on his bottom lip, continuing the stroking of that jewel between her thick thighs. He glanced at his veined dick, sliding in and out of her shaven vagina, admiring what looked like shampoo on his manhood. Feeling her pussy muscles tightened around him, his eyes shot open and he looked down. Her pussy was oozing more of that white shit and her face was a mask of pleasure. Her lips were trembling, as she attempted to say something.

"Baeeee, you feeeeel sooo goood, ooooh, Pa," she whined. "Uhh! Uhh! Uhh! Uhh!"

"Uhh! Uhh! Uhh! Uhh!" He stared her right in her pleasured face, diving in and out of her womb. Her insides squeezing his rod increased the intensity of the sex for him, and he felt himself about to rupture. All this did was drive him to pick up the pace and, before long, the bed was squeaking and rocking, head board banging up against the wall.

"Ah! Ah! Ah! Ah! Ah!" she hollered out.

"Uh! Uh! Uh! Ooooh, shit. I'ma 'bout to cum, bae. Shit, this pussy good. You got some good pussy, O. Damn, ma!"

"You… you got some good diiiick!"

"Ahhhh, I'm 'bouta nut! Unhhhh!" A look of relief swept over his face as he busted all inside of Odette. He bit down on his inner jaw and continued to stoke her, oozing more of his penis' semen inside of her hole. He filled her up to the rim and his essence came spilling out of her slit, soiling the comforter that they laid upon. She motioned for him to lean over to her and she grasped his face, kissing him hard and deep. He kissed her on her neck and face. Pulling back, they stared into one another's tearing eyes, until finally wetness came running down their cheeks. They cried and told one another over and over again that they 'loved' the other, all the while kissing.

Kreon fell on top of Odette and shut his eyelids. She shut hers as well, rubbing him up and down his back until they both drifted off to sleep.

***

Jaekwon crossed the threshold of Denny's, pushing open one of its glass doors. He was in a Cardinals fitted cap, which he wore low over his brows and a hood that he had covering it. The nigga even went so far as to wear a patch over his left eye and fake beard so that anyone that knew him wouldn't recognize him. The last thing he wanted was to run into one of his homies and have them notice him at a sit down with a couple federal agents. Hell, if that was to happen, he knew that he may as well excuse himself to the men's room and swallow a bullet. *That's right. Kill his mothafucking self!*

"How many, sir?" A young petite white woman approached Jaekwon, smiling. This was one of the waitresses at the establishment. She had an ink pen behind her ear and was holding a couple of laminated menus. When she'd approached, Jaekwon was looking around suspiciously for any familiar faces, hands shoved in the pockets of his hoodie. He was too busy scoping out the area to have acknowledged her, so the sound of her voice had startled him. On edge, he started to go for the Beretta tucked on his hip, but that's when he remembered where he was and who he was there to meet.

"Uh, a table for three, please." He threw up three fingers. "I'm here to see two nigg… I mean, two friends of mine. There white gentlemen. One tall with reddish orange hair and the otha bald." He used his hand to describe what the federal agents' hairstyles looked like.

"Sssssssss," the young white woman hissed and narrowed her eyelids, tilting her head aside. "I'm sorry, but no one that looks like those two guys have been here, 'less they came before my shift. And I started six hours ago."

Jaekwon pulled back the sleeve of his hoodie and glanced at his Rolex. Seeing that it was fifteen minutes after the meeting time, he took another look around the restaurant to see if he'd see the men in question. When he didn't see Detectives Burton and Bland, he focused his attention back on the waitress and took a deep breath.

"Okay, show me to a table of three. If you see my two friends that I described, send 'em to whatever table you seat me at."

"You got it. Come with me." She motioned for him to follow her. She showed him to a table, which he declined, wishing to be seated a table far over in the corner where he could see everyone coming and going through the doors.

Once Jaekwon was seated, the waitress sat a menu down before him and asked him what he would like to drink. He said the first thing that came into his mind, which was water. Afterwards, he opened the menu and ordered up the first thing that his eyes landed on and handed the menu back over.

"Okay. One Honey Jalapeno Bacon Sriracha Burger coming right up." The waitress scribbled down what he wanted to eat. She then flashed him a toothy smile, picked up his menu, and went on about her business.

It wasn't long before the waitress came back with Jaekwon's glass of water and a straw. He thanked her and tilted the brim of his cap, sending her off. He took a sip of the water and opened the straw, sitting the torn white paper aside. He then played the cool role at the back of Denny's, placing the straw in his mouth and gnawing on it.

Jaekwon had gotten pulled over with a couple of kilos of cocaine and a Beretta. Fearing all the time that he was facing, he hopped out of his car, firing at the cop that pulled him over. He took the officer off his feet but, luckily, he was wearing a bulletproof vest. Although the law enforcer had been gunned down, he managed to take a shot at Jaekwon. The bullet grounded him and broke his arm, leaving him wearing a cast up until today.

Facing more time than he was willing to do, Jaekwon made a deal to go undercover as an informant for the F.B.I., to gather evidence to bring his uncle Omar and his empire down. The nigga had been throwing The Alphabet Boys information here and there. But, it wasn't enough to bury his uncle for as long as they'd like to, so they let him continue to do his thing until they had something on him that would guarantee that he'd never see daylight again.

The Feds gifted Jaekwon with a gold chain that operated as a camera and a recording device. The young nigga was to wear it to get visuals of anything that may help them build a case against his people. Now, this was where the problem came in. The night that Jaekwon was supposed to turn the camera on, the chain *on* it malfunctioned. This was bad because he couldn't film the murder that he, Omar, and Kreon put down on Khadafi. He wasn't too disappointed though. This was because he was involved in the murder and he didn't want the Feds knowing that he had a hand in the priest meeting his Maker.

Jaekwon was posted up at Denny's now, to give Detectives Burton and Bland all the information that he'd gathered since the last time that he'd seen them. He was also going to break the news of the murder that occurred, but he wasn't going to tell them about his involvement. He was sure that if he breathed a word of it, they would lock his ass up for all of eternity. They couldn't be too mad about him not getting any footage on the Khadafi's murder though. Hell, it wasn't his fault that their piece of shit chain malfunctioned.

Jaekwon looked at the burger that sat before him. The beef patty had grown cold and its buns were stale. Having grown tired of waiting for the agents, Jaekwon took a deep breath and pulled out the cellular given to him by the F.B.I. He flipped it open with his thumb and speed dialed the number given to him. Placing the cellular to his ear, he listened to it ring three times before Agent Bland answered.

"Yo', Bland, where y'all niggaz at, man?" Jaekwon asked annoyed.

"Keep your blouse on, sweetheart; we'll be there in a second." Bland responded and disconnected the call before

Jaekwon could respond.   "Punk ass nigga." Jaekwon snapped his federal issued cell phone closed and rose from his seat, stashing the device inside the pocket of his hoodie. Pulling out a healthy wad of dead presidents from his Levi's, he peeled off a twenty-dollar bill and dropped it on the table top. He then picked up his glass of water and sat it down on top of the bill before making his exit.

Heading towards his Infinity truck, Jaekwon broke the cellphone in half and threw it inside of the gutter. He then opened the driver's door of his SUV and hopped in behind the wheel, slamming the door shut. As soon as he cranked up his vehicle, The Relativez' *Like That* came thumping through the truck's sound system. He threw the gear shift into drive and sped off, the music's high volume rattling the Infinity.

Jaekwon cracked open the window as he took pulls from his blunt, staring ahead. The wind invaded the vehicle, ruffling the young nigga'z clothing and blowing embers from the burning end of his bleezy.

Fuck the F.B.I.; I'm not doin' this snitch shit no mo'. They gone have to catch me when they can and, even if they do, fuck it, blood! I'll swallow a bullet before I see the inside of a cage, on mommas. Jaekwon switched hands with the blunt and picked up his gun, lying it down in his lap.

Later that night

Odette's eyelids flickered opened and she found herself staring at a sleeping Kreon. A smile broadened her face and she scooted closer to him, playing with the hair on his chest. Having done that, she kissed his lips and began placing a hickey on his neck, trying to wake him up for another round of sex. Suddenly, his eyelids flickered open and he made a hideous face, eyes pooling with tears. He sat straight up in bed, embracing either side of his head with his hands and balling up his face.

"Why did you wake me up?" he screamed on Odette, tears running down his face as he breathed heavily. His hairy chest jumped up and down hurriedly. His nostrils throbbed and he twisted his lips. Heatedly, he looked around for his clothing. The nigga was pissed off about his sleep being disturbed.

Worry etched across Odette's face, as she tried to figure out why he was so pissed off. She'd always played around with him while he slept. Normally, he'd wake up and they'd play fight and end up making out.

"I don't understand… why are you so angry?" Her forehead was crinkled as she watched him get dressed.

"Cause you broke my sleep," he responded angrily, slipping on his blue and white basketball shorts. He took the time to slip on a pair of socks and then turned to her. She couldn't see his eyes in the dark, but they were glassy and on the verge of tears. "Do you know, besides alcohol, that sleep is my only escape from it?"

"Escape from what?" she curiously inquired.

"From what's going on up here." He tapped his temple and slipped his feet inside of his corduroy house shoes. Afterwards, he left the bedroom before she could see his hurt spilling down his cheeks. He'd left his car keys and cellphone behind, so she knew he wasn't going too far, if anywhere for that matter. She just knew that he didn't want to be in the same space as her right then.

Kreon laid on his side on the couch and squeezed his eyelids shut. It wasn't long before he was gritting and tears were sliding down his cheeks. No matter how many times he tried to explain to his loved ones how important his sleep was to him, it seemed like they never understood or they thought he was overexaggerating. You know, trying to juice his illness for sympathy. That wasn't the case at all though. He felt like fuck anyone who thought that was what he was trying to do that. They didn't know what it was like to be him? So, how the fuck could they say what he was feeling?

He knew at that moment that the only people that would understand what it was like to be him were the ones exactly like him. Even his fucking therapist didn't know. And, how could he? To tell someone what something is like was one thing, but for them to experience it was an entirely different aspect. None of that mattered now, though. He had bigger fish to fry, like the drama currently occupying his mind. It was his alone to deal with… just like it had always been.

Kreon gritted further and squeezed his eyelids shut even tighter, wrinkling his entire face. His form slightly shook, as he combated that eerie feeling inside of his brain. His body felt hot and he could feel all the veins bulging on him. He was so engrossed with his opponent that he didn't hear the bedroom door squeak open, and Odette tip toe out into the living room. Her forehead crinkled further, watching him battle his demons. Although she loved him, she knew that she'd never understand him, but she'd always try. A lone tear descended her chocolate cheek as she stood partially out of the entrance of the living room.

Feeling that she had to do something to help her man, she tightened her robe on her and stepped inside of the living room. Cautiously, she crept towards him until she was on top of him, her shadow looming over him. As he continued to shake, she outstretched her hand to touch his head but thought against doing so, for fear of setting him off again. Withdrawing her hand, she looked up to the ceiling and said a silent prayer for God to cover her man in his blood and to look out for him. With that having been done, she crept back to the bedroom and laid upon it like Kreon was on the couch.

Unbeknownst to them, they were both sobbing, Kreon because he was exhausted with fighting to stay alive, and Odette because she felt like she wasn't doing enough in helping him in his struggle.

***

Po and his niggaz played the staircase in front of the apartment complex, passing a bleezy between them and shooting the breeze. Occasionally, a crackhead would come up and purchase crack from him. Po would take the money and hold his fist to his mouth, blowing a rock or two inside of it, then passing it off to the fiend that was copping from him. The night was cool, so you could see the white smoke whenever homeboy and anyone out of his crew breathe.

Po had just served a fiend when a three Crown Victoria's swooped in, tires screeching to a halt. Plain clothes detectives jumped out holding guns, startling Po and his crew. Seeing no place for them to run, they threw their hands up in the air. The law moved in and patted everyone down, once they were handcuffed. Their pat down produced firearms and crack. Po looked up to the window of the unit that Kreon resided in. He was just in time to see Ella snatching her head away, curtain falling back over it.

"Fuckin' snitch, you mothafuckin' snitch ass bitch!" Spit flew from off his big lips as his head was pushed down, shoved into the backseat of the car. The detective slammed the door shut and hopped in behind the wheel, driving off. The other unmarked cars were right behind it, leaving the front of the complex quiet, except for the sounds of the crickets.

CHAPTER FIVE
A couple days later

Hot water sprayed from the showerhead, pelting the tiled wall and slicking the inside of the tub. Slowly, a fog manifested that rolled across the floor and up the walls, bringing up the temperature. Kreon stood before the medicine cabinet's mirror, looking over his reflection. His form shined from the humidity inside of the bathroom. The young man was as naked as the day his mother had pushed him from out of her womb into this God forsaken world. Never would he begin to think that he would face all that he had in the twenty something odd years he'd been alive. If you would have told him that he'd survive all that he did, he wouldn't believe you either. But, here he was, living proof of his trial and tribulations. And although he was marred and scarred, he was still above ground, where most niggaz lying in the cemetery wish they were.

Kreon's body was more flawed than anyone's. He had cigarette burns on the back of his neck and down his back from his father using him as a human ashtray, a nasty scar that travel up his belly and left his navel at a funny angle from a surgery he had after being shot in a drive by, an ugly scar inside the palm of his hand where he'd been stabbed in a street fight, and an extension cord burn around his neck from when he tried to hang himself to escape his father's abuse. It was safe to say that old Kreon wouldn't know an easy day of living if he saw one.

Kreon picked up his iPod from off the edge of the sink and searched through it until he found the mix tracks he was looking for. Having programmed the playlist to play what he desired, he sat the silver and black device back down from where he'd picked it up from. Before he knew it, Goapele's *Closer* came flowing from the speakers. This was one of his favorite songs. He could listen to it repeatedly.

Closer to my dreams

I'm goin' higher and higher
I ain't gonna sleep
Sometimes, you just have to let it go (Let it go, let it go)
Leaving all my fears to burn down
Push them all away so I can move on

Kreon turned around from the medicine cabinet's mirror and approached the shower's sliding door. He'd just pulled it open when a knock at the door drew his attention, causing him to look over his shoulder.

"What's up?" he called out.

"It's me, bae. Can I come in?"

"I don't know, can you?"

She chuckled and said, "*May I* come in?"

"It's a free country."

Right then, the bathroom door came open and a smiling Odette entered, pulling the door shut behind her. She was in a black silk robe.

"I thought I'd join you," she said, pulling the ends loose that held her robe on her. As soon as they came free, Kreon was captured by her coconut-shaped breasts, hips, and thighs. What stood out most about her body were the small, extra nipples that were higher up on both tits and the silky hairs of her mound, which were cut to form an upside down Egyptian pyramid. Her beautiful chocolate skin was damn near flawless, and her individual braids were pulled back and wrapped up to form a bun. She wasn't ashamed of her body any longer. Nah, Kreon had made her completely comfortable with it. She'd forever love his ass for that.

Kreon cracked a smile as he approached her, dick and balls hanging. He slipped the robe from off Odette's shoulders and it fell into a pile at her manicured feet. He then kissed her slow and tenderly before grabbing her hand and leading her over to the tub. He allowed her to step inside of the tub first and, then, he came in behind her, pulling the sliding door shut.

Seeing Kreon about to pick up the loofa, Odette hurried up and picked it up before he could.

"Let me get that for you, my king." She smiled, picking up the Dove body wash from the corner of the porcelain tub. After she squeezed some of the foamy substance into the loofa, she sat the body-wash down from where she'd gotten it and motioned for Kreon to turn back around. The young man obliged her and turned around, placing one hand up against the tiled wall while the other hung at his side. Shutting his eyelids and bowing his head, he took a deep breath and relaxed.

"You ever had a woman bathe you before?" Odette inquired, lathering her man up with the loofa. The corner of her mouth curled with a smirk. If it wasn't anything that she loved to do, it was pleasing the man that she was with. In doing so, she got an amazing high. It was something about holding down her man and proving that she was worthy of him that put her on cloud 9.

"Nah, consider yourself lucky. I never allow anyone to get as close to me as you are right now. I always suspect 'em to stab me in the back," he stated emotionless, swiping the water from off his face with a sweep of his palm.

Odette's forehead wrinkled hearing her boo's response. "You mean, you don't trust people?"

"Notta soul."

"Why is that?"

"Cause everyone that I have ever loved, includin' my motha, has hurt me. So, you gotta excuse me if I'm not as willing as otha people to be trustin' niggaz and shit."

"I hear you, but you gotta trust someone."

"I do, slim."

"Oh yeah? Well, who's that?"

"The realest nigga in the world… me. There's no one else outside of that."

"What about me?" she asked, still soaping him up with the loofa.

He was silent for a second before responding, "I trust you to a certain extent. The rest has to be earned over time."

"I feel you. Well, I trust you."

"Is that right?"

"Yes."

"Why do you trust me?"

"I don't know really. I guess it's because I feel so safe around you. You give off this aura that's so cool and calm. You're very mellow. Truthfully, there's nothing about you not to trust... so, I guess it's safe to say that's why I trust you."

"Great answer."

Odette bent down, lathering up Kreon's calves and legs. While doing this, she watched as the suds slid off his legs and rolled towards the drain, swirling down at it.

"Thanks."

For a couple of moments, there was silence, as she carried out the task of washing him up.

"Babe, I was just thinking, I know so little about what you been through. I mean, I know you've faced some hardships, but I don't actually know what they are. You've never went into detail like I have, is what I'm saying."

"Growing up, I was abused mentally and physically. Not only by the man I was led to believe was my father, but by other mothafuckaz too."

"See, babe, now we're getting somewhere."

"I'm don't wanna chop that shit up, O. All a nigga know is the shit that I been through in life has fucked me up. I feel like I'll never be able to get right. It's like... it's like there's this black hole right in the center of me, and no amount of money, love, sex, or drugs can fill it," he said, tearing up. "I'm hurtin' inside, really, really bad, and I don't know how to stop it. The only thing that I can think of is death, killin' myself. Stickin' my pistol inside my grill and pullin' the trigga." He became silent, staring ahead at nothing, just thinking. "You know what the crazy part about it is?"

"No, what's that?" Odette asked, still soaping him up with her loofa.

"I don't even want to die. It's just that I know that if I ever do… this withering pain that I'm feelin' inside will finally be gone, once and for all." Unbeknownst to him, she was crying, soaping him up slower now. She hated hearing about him dying. It fucked her up. He was the love of her life and she didn't want anything to happen to him… ever.

"Baby, please stop talking like that, please." She pressed her face against his sudsy back and embraced him from his rear, tears treading down her face. "Every time you start talking like that, I get petrified. I don't want anything to ever happen to you, boo. That shit scares me, it scares me to death." She whimpered and trembled against him. Teary-eyed, he looked over his shoulder and grabbed the lower half of her back to comfort her.

"Alright, no more talk about dying. I'ma try…" He looked up at the ceiling, tears threatening to fall from the rims of his eyes. As soon as he shut his eyelids, tears jetted down his cheeks. "I'ma try to just focus on livin' and getting better. If I keep speaking negatively, then I'ma stay in the predicament that I'm in with this shit." He peeled his eyelids back open and took a deep breath. Swallowing the extra spit in his mouth, his throat slid up and down his neck. He then shut his eyelids again and tilted his head down, allowing his woman to finish soaping him up.

Once she was done, his entire body was masked white with soap bubbles scattered all over him. Leaning his head back again, he let Odette shampoo his hair and, then, he bowed. When he did this, his head came into contact with the spraying hot water from the showerhead, rinsing the shampoo from out of his hair. Odette massaged his scalp as the force of the liquid pelted it, helping rinse the chemical from out of his hair. Once the shampoo was out of her man's hair, Odette conditioned it and then washed the soap from off his form. Seeing that she was finished, Kreon recovered the loofa from her and soaped his woman up. Afterwards, he shampooed and conditioned her hair, rinsing it thoroughly.

Once Odette was good and clean, he instructed her to grab her ankles. She didn't ask any questions, she did just it. Getting down on his knees, Kreon parted her buttocks and held them open. His view from behind her was of her tight asshole and her fat, shaven vagina. Sticking out his tongue, he pressed it between the beginnings of her pussy lips and slid it up and down its full length. Coming back to her swollen clit, he flicked it with his tongue rapidly, causing her to convulse and her eyes to roll back to their whites. He then sucked on the small flap of meat nestled between her southern lips; she moaned, wearing a mask of pleasure. Her face seemed to be stuck with her eyes rolled back and her mouth hanging open. Feeling her pull away from him, he grabbed her by her wrists and pulled her arms back a little, holding her in place. His eyelids were shut as he continued to devour the flap of meat, slobbering and sucking on it expertly.

"Ooooh, right there, Papi! Ooooooooh, yes, yesss, right fucking there! Don't stop! Sssssss, that's right, eat cho mothafucking pussy, boy! Eat it up!"

"You like that shit?" he asked her between eating her pussy.

"Oh yes, yes, I love it!" she whined, eyelids flickering and flashing the whites of her eyes. "I fucking love it!" Abruptly, her eyelids stretched wide open and she gasped. Her form shook uncontrollably and she squirted fast and furiously. He told her to stay in that same position that she was in, holding her ankles while bent over. His dick grew harder than average and veins bulged throughout it, penis head throbbing. He grabbed his manhood and swiped up and down the crack of her ass as the shower's water beat down upon them both, rolling down their respective forms. Slowly, he guided himself in between her warm, gooey walls and felt her snugness accept him upon entrée. Gripping her meaty hips, he threw his head back and narrowed his eyelids, gently sliding his hardness in and out her. He began to pick up speed and his pelvis smacked up against her buttocks thunderously. The bathroom filled with his grunts and her whines of pleasure. The white lather from her V slicked his dick, but the spraying showerhead washed it from off his manhood.

"Ooooh, get it! Get this pussy! It's your, papi! All of it!" she winced with her eyelids squeezed shut, lips quivering from ecstasy. She enjoyed how full she felt from the width of his manliness, pummeling her treasure into submission.

"This my shit?" he asked, slamming into her aggressively. He smacked her hard on her ass and sent a ripple through it. It stung her, but it felt so good. Sometimes, she liked that rough ass sex. Gripping her respective butt cheeks and holding them apart, he looked down as he dove himself in and out of her slick, pink tunnel.

"Yes, this your pussy, baby! Fuck me! Fuck your pussy and make it come!" Odette's pussy muscles contracted and held fast, trying to make it difficult for him to get in and out of her V. Glancing down for a moment, Kreon saw her ball up her toes. This let him know that she was close to coming. Acknowledging this, he sped up his stroking and smacked her ass cheeks harder, leaving red hand impressions behind.

Smack! Smack! Smack! Smack!

Kreon grunted and gripped her hips tighter, running that raw dick up in her shaved twat. He felt his hairy nut sack swell up and the head of his penis enlarged. It wouldn't be long before he busted.

"Aaaah!" He threw his head back and licked his full lips, smacking her big black ass once again. The pussy was immaculate, and he felt like as if he could fuck her forever. "Aaaaah, ah shit! Here I come!" He looked back down at his manhood jabbing her middle feverishly, gritting his teeth. "Here I come in this mothafuckin' pussy. I'm bouta… I'm bouta fill this bitch up, girl!"

"Fill her up, fill your mothafucking pussy up!" Her face winced further and her lips trembled out of control. Her thick thighs shook as she felt herself about to orgasm again.

"You ready for it, baby?" His eyebrows sloped and his nose scrunched up, muscles shown in his face as he clenched his jaws tight. He was ramming her so hard from the back that she was lurching forth and nearly falling every time their bodies collided.

"Yes, I'm ready, daddy! Nut all up in this pussy!" she commanded.

He gripped her hips even tighter and slammed up inside of her pussy four more times. Holding himself inside of her womb on the fourth slam, he unleashed all his hot, gooey baby batter inside of her. Feeling his seeds splash inside of her sacred hole, she came right after him and shook. Weak in the knees, she nearly fell afterwards, so she grabbed upon the slick walls and turned around to him. She threw her mouth against his and they kissed long, deep, and hard. While they were locking lips, she stroked his semi erect dick, making sure every last drop of his kids had been freed from captivity.

They stood erect inside of the tub, wrapped in one another's arms, kissing like lovers do, shower water pelting their wet bodies.

Later that day

The weather was perfect. It was fairly hot with the occasional breeze keeping people cool. The fiery-orange ball, known as the sun, beat down on all the kids in the hood. The air was filled with adolescent voices, as well as the much younger ones of children. At this time, they were all playing ghetto baseball in the middle of the street. They couldn't afford a bat and a baseball, so they substituted these items with a broken broom handle and a soft ball about the same size of a real baseball. A lot of the kids participating wore the caps and knock off jerseys of their favorite baseball players. The little niggaz were also chewing bubble gum and spitting off to the side, treating it like it was real chewing tobacco. The catcher's mitt they wore were either tattered or a couple of sizes too big, but they didn't give a fuck though. They were having the time of their young lives and they weren't about to allow anyone to ruin it.

Next up to bat was one of the only white kids of the neighborhood. He was eight years old and had long, stringy blond hair that spilled out from under his Angels baseball cap, which he wore backwards. His left jaw was swollen with bubble gum, making it appear as if it was tobacco that he was actually chewing. Picking up the broom stick, he tapped the heels of his sneakers to rid himself of the imaginary dirt that was on the bottoms of them. He them got into a batting position, practicing swinging the stick like one of the pros in the sport. A hefty Asian kid by the name of Pie, which he'd gotten from his round face played the umpire, squatting low behind the white kid that was up to bat.

Felipe was a tall, thick Mexican youth. He was the only child in the street that was wearing the real replica of his favorite player's baseball jersey. The youngster was one of the acting pitchers and he was actually good at his position. This was probably because he was taught by his father, who used to pitch professionally for the Kansas City Royals before he was kicked off the team for testing positive for steroids.

Felipe chewed gum and punched the softball into his catcher's mitt as he stood upright. He was waiting for the next batter to step to the plate. Once the batter, a white kid with long blonde hair, approached the plate, he practiced swinging the stick before getting into position. Once he saw that the Caucasian boy was ready, he took the signal from the umpire and then threw the ball. The ball ripped through the air, en route to the kid behind the stick. Seeing the ball flying towards him, the boy swung with all his might. The stick whistled through the air and completely missed the ball.

The ball was caught by the umpire with ease. The heavy-set umpire smiled and nodded to the pitcher.

While all of this was taking place, Kreon was sitting on a chair on the front porch, Odette straddled on his lap. They were behaving like a couple of teenage lovers stowed away somewhere under the bleachers. They were staring into one another's eyes lovingly pecking and kissing affectionately. Anyone on the outside looking in could tell that the two loved one another. Kreon and Odette had the biggest smiles stretched across their lips and were glowing.

Odette's head was in the clouds; she was so far gone over Kreon. A nigga had her feeling like this since… well, a nigga had never had her feeling like this. And she loved it. She absolutely loved it. No one could tell her that homeboy wasn't the one for her and that they weren't destined to be together. Little momma saw her entire future with him. The girl could literally see it playing out before her eyes, like she was sitting in the middle of the theater stuffing her mouth with popcorn, watching it. This was a movie, her movie. And she never wanted to see the end credits, no matter how great the film's ending was.

"You love me?" Kreon asked, staring deep into those brown orbs with the black dots in the middle of them that were Odette's eyes. His meaty hands were gripping her ample bottom, imprinting themselves in the fabric of her leggings.

"Yep," she stated proudly with a smile.

"You betta 'cause if you didn't, I'd kick yo' chocolate ass."

"Shut up and kiss me," she chuckled and kissed him. Wrapping her arms around his neck, she leaned forward, kissing him deep and passionately.

"Thank you," he said to her while staring into her eyes, looking serious.

"For what?" she wondered, forehead creased.

"Loving me."

"Aawww, you made it so easy."

He blushed and replied, "Seriously though. Thanks."

"No problem, slim," she mocked him and he laughed. "But, you owe me one."

"What I owe you, beautiful?" He swept the individual braids out of her face and tucked them behind her ear.

"A happily ever after, Mr. Williams."

"One happily ever after, you got it, Ms. Dante?" Kreon caressed the side of her face with the side of his hand.

She grasped his wrist and kissed the palm of his hand, rubbing her cheek against it affectionately. "Marry me?"

"You serious?" He cracked a one-sided grin.

"Unh hunh." She nodded.

Still grinning, he threw his head back and said, "This dick must be fiiiiyah!"

She playfully punched him and looked him square in his eyes. "I'm serious."

"You are serious." He realized, after examining the look written across her face.

"As serious as I've ever been about anyth…"

The eruptions of children's hoots and hollers filled the air and drew the couple's attention. Odette climbed off Kreon and they both stood up, looking out into the street. The white kid wearing the backwards cap had finally hit the ball. He had taken off running, leaving the opposing team scrambling to get the ball, which was bouncing down the street. The ball eventually rolled underneath a parked van and bumped up against the curb, settling there. By the time one of the players of the opposing team got the ball, the white kid had already stolen home plate.

"Mommy, Kreon, I'm next up!" Marquise called out from where he was on the sidewalk, along with the rest of the kids who were waiting for their chance to hit the ball. The little dude was dressed in a Dodgers baseball cap and t-shirt with the famous team's logo emblazoned on the front of it. The boy ran out into the street and picked up the broom handle, practicing swinging it like the lad before him.

"Come on." Odette tapped Kreon and they ran outside of the yard onto the sidewalk, so they could watch the game. They placed their hands above their brows to block the rainbow rays shining in their faces. The shadows of their hands were casted over their faces and they were squinting their eyelids from the intense illumination of the sun. "Come on." She clapped her hands cheerfully. "Show them what chu got, baby boy; knock that sucker out of the neighborhood!"

"Let's get that home run, slim, blast that mothafuck…" Kreon stopped his clapping and cheering when Odette shot him an evil eye and nudged him. "What?" He shrugged and looked at her with a raised eyebrow like, *what the hell is the matter with you?*

"Don't be cussing around him, babe. He's very impressionable. He'll pick up everything you say and be reciting it like a goddamn parrot." she told him this in a hushed tone, still clapping her hands.

"Oh, my fault, I gotchu. I'll try to watch my mouth around lil' dude."

"That's all I ask, thanks handsome." She gave him a quick peck on the lips and they continued to clap and cheer Marquise on.

Felipe blew a huge pink bubble out of his gum and it exploded. He smacked the ball into his catcher's mitt a few times before hiking up a leg, twisting his body and flinging his arm forward. He released the ball from his palm so fast that it ripped through the air, appearing as if it was leaving a trail of fire behind it. Marquise swung the stick and missed the ball. He heard the impact of the ball as it landed into the umpire's catcher's mitt. The boy gritted his teeth and stomped his foot, angry that he'd struck out.

Grim expressions cross Odette and Kreon's faces, seeing the youngster get struck out.

"It's okay, baby boy. It's okay, you still got two more tries." Odette clapped and attempted to motivate her son.

"That ain't about nothing, Y.G. you'll get it; don't even trip. You just concentrate on knocking that ball into outer space. You Griff me?" Kreon gave him motivation.

Marquise nodded, hearing his mother and her boyfriend. He slid his feet into position and lifted the broom stick above his shoulders as if it were a baseball bat.

Swoooooop!

The stick whistled through the air, completely missing the ball. It was followed by a *Pact!* Which was the sound that the ball made when the umpire caught it inside of his catcher's mitt.

Odette whipped her head away from her son. Pissed off, she said fucked in a harsh, hushed tone, "Fuck!" Kreon looked at her and grinned, reminded of her telling him to watch his mouth in front of her son. "Shut up, bae!" she smirked and playfully punched him in the arm.

Still grinning he said, "I ain't say nothin'."

"You were thinking it." Odette smiled as he kissed her cheek.

Kreon focused on a frustrated Marquise. In doing so, he envisioned him swinging the stick over and over again. His eyebrows rose and his eyes bugged when he realized the flaw in the boy's swinging of his homemade baseball bat. Everything clicked like the trigger of a gun to him, and he knew right then what the youngster should do.

Hoots and hollers of the children filled the air once again, as Marquise readied himself for Felipe's hood famous fastball. A sinister smile spread across the Mexican youth's face, showcasing his top row of shiny, silver teeth. The sunlight hit his grill and a small rainbow deflected off it.

Kreon cupped his hands around his mouth. "Don't swing it forward, Marquise! You gotta get up unda the ball…" he called out to the little dude to get his attention, and he looked at him. It was then that he gripped an imaginary baseball bat and showed him how to swing his stick at the ball. "Like that, okay? You gotta get up unda that mothafucka and crack it, alright?" He looked at Odette from the corner of his eyes to see what she would say to his cussing again. He didn't mean to cuss again. It was just how his ass talked.

"I'm going to let that one slide, since it could help him," she told him.

"My bad, you know it's all love this way." He cracked a smile and pulled her closer to him with one arm, looking deep into her eyes. She smiled back at him, caressing the side of his face with the palm of her petite hand.

"I know." She batted her eyelashes, continuing to smile. "But please, please, please try to watch your mouth around him."

"Anything for you, baby." He kissed her twice on the lips and smacked her on the ass once she turned around to finish watching the game.

Damn, Mocha, gotta big ol' ass, he openly admired her backside, biting down on his curled finger. He then focused his attention back on the game. He found Marquise practice-swinging his stick, visualizing himself knocking the baseball high and far across the sky.

Felipe cocked back the hand that held the ball and threw it forward, releasing the baseball. The ball seemed to be flying at its regular speed toward Marquise, but the boy saw it moving in slow motion. In fact, everything in his sight was in black and white, except the baseball; it was its original color. *Blue!* The only thing that the youth could hear was his breathing and the sound of his heart beating fast. Sweat trickled from his brow and he clenched his jaws tight, gripping the stick tighter. Although the ball was spinning in his direction getting closer and closer, it was still flying slowly at him. Taking Kreon's advice, Marquise clenched his jaws tighter and got up under the fast ball with his stick. He swung his stick with all his might, squeezing his eyelids shut while doing it. Upon impact with the stick, the ball made a loud noise that echoed throughout the neighborhood. The ball looked like a blur, as it rocketed high across the sky en route to an entirely different urban community. Kreon, Odette, and the children looked up at the ball in awe, eyes bulging and mouths wide open.

"Oh my God, my baby hit a home run!" Odette screamed and hollered, jumping up and down while clapping her hands. With surprised expressions on their faces, she and Kreon looked at Marquise. The boy had the exact same surprised expression across his face, only he was looking at the stick as if it had mystical powers.

"Run, Marquise, run!" Odette and Kreon yelled out to the youngster.

Marquise looked back and forth between his mother and her boyfriend and the stick. It was then that he snapped out of it and threw the stick down, taking off running to all the bases. The neighborhood kids cheered him on as he made his rounds. Nearing home plate, he did *The Harlem Shake* and strolled over to the plate, jumping down upon it while throwing his baseball cap high into the air. At that moment, the children mobbed him, showing him love and giving him praise. Kreon hoisted the little nigga over his shoulders and walked him around victoriously. Marquise couldn't stop smiling; he'd never felt more proud or excited in the short time he'd been alive.

Kreon sat Marquise down and addressed the children while rubbing his hands together, he said, "Alright, everybody, pizza and we watchin' Sing at Aunty O's house." He looked at her and she was frowning. Noticing that the kids were looking at her, she smiled and agreed to have them at her house.

"I'm going to give your butt a wedgie for that one," she smirked and pointed at him.

"That's a small price to pay for my lil' homie's happiness." Kreon looked down at his lady's son and ruffled his hair. The boy smiled at him and he smiled back.

That night

All the children from the baseball game earlier that day sat on the living room floor, stuffing their faces with pizza and drinking red plastic cups of soda. They laughed and smiled at *Sing,* which was playing on the 42-inch flat-screen; its blue rays flashing across their young faces as they were being entertained. Kreon sat on the Lay-Z-Boy chair, with Odette cuddled up against him underneath a plaid blanket. Smiles were plastered on their faces as they watched the children enjoying themselves. Most noticeably among them was Marquise, who was holding a conversation among his peers and occasionally glancing at the screen. It was evident to Kreon and Odette that the youngster was delighted by his friends.

"Look at him, babe. He's so happy." Odette pointed her son out among the children, smiling.

"Yeah, I see 'em, happier than a fag with a bag full of dicks." Kreon smiled from ear to ear, watching young Marquise.

"I'm so happy for him," she said, snuggling up against Kreon and shutting her eyelids, grin etched across her face.

"Me too." He kissed the top of her head and focused back on the tv. Seeing someone at the corner of his eye, he looked and found Marquise advancing in his direction. The little boy crawled upon him and hugged him, pressing his cheek up against his while smiling. This caused Kreon to blush. He wasn't big on affection, so it made him feel funny inside having someone so open with displaying theirs. At that moment, he realized that displays of affection were something that the kid and his mother didn't have any problems with.

"What was that for?" he smirked, looking at the boy.

"For helping me hit that homer today. I couldn't have done it without you."

"Nah, lil' dude." He ruffled his hair. "You've always had it in you, I just gave you a lil' guidance is all."

"Nah." He shook his head. "I'm sure if it wasn't for you that I wouldn't have hit that ball as far as I did. So, thank you."

"You welcome, lil' homie." He rubbed the top of the boy's head and stared him in his eyes. It was then that he saw the innocence in the youth. He also saw the way he was looking at him. He was looking at him like he was his hero, like he was larger than life and he wanted to do nothing more than to be just like him when he grew it. This was the same way that a younger Kreon had looked at his Grandpa Joe and his Uncle Omar. They were everything that he aspired to be growing up. Although he didn't ask to be Marquise's role model, he was going to try his best to one worthy of looking up to for as long as he lived. "Gone... gone finish watchin' yo' show with yo' lil' homeboys, alright?"

"Alright."

"Hold up," he called him back as he was about to walk off. When the boy turned around, he outstretched his fist toward him. "Gone hit that rock, lil' nigga."

Marquise smiled and touched fist with Kreon. He then joined back up with his neighborhood friends, watching *Sing*.

CHAPTER SIX
An hour later

Marquise stood beside Kreon, who was holding open the front door while watching the children as they filed out over the threshold. As the children crossed their paths, they high-fived them and continued out of the door, some of them wearing pasta stains from the pizza they ate earlier.

"Good game." a shorter boy said to Marquise, giving him a high-five.

"Good game," a taller boy said to him, high-fiving him.

"What a hit!" a girl said to him, giving him a high-five.

The last three kids gave Marquise his props before hitting Kreon's rock (his fist) and heading on out of the door. When he shut the door behind them and turned around, a broom and dust pan was thrown at him. He caught them both and looked up frowning, wondering who'd thrown the household items at him. He was surprised to see Odette standing not too far from him, stacking empty Little Caesars pizza boxes.

"Time to clean up, Big Daddy," Odette announced.

Kreon looked over the living room. It definitely needed to be cleaned up. There were empty and half-empty plastic cups, crumbs, and abandoned paper plates scattered all over the living room.

"Well." Marquise yawned and stretched his arms, hearing his own bones cracking. "I'm as tired as a runaway slave. I'll see y'all in the morning; love you, ma, love you, Kreon." He waved goodbye to them and walked toward his bedroom. He'd gotten halfway there when his mother grabbed him by the collar of his shirt, jerking him to a stop. The boy turned around with furrowed brows.

"Not so fast, little man, you gone help around here. It was your company that made this mess, so you're going to pitch in."

"Awww, ma, I'm sleepy," he complained.

"Well, your little butt better get un-tired, here." She passed him a black garbage bag, which was partially full of trash from the gathering. "Walk around and stuff whatever trash you see inside of this bag and place it into the garbage outside."

"Come on, mom," he pouted.

"Come on, mom, my ass; get cho little black butt on task. Gone." She swatted him on his ass. Her small assault lurched the little dude forward, but he went on to do as he was told. When Odette looked up, she saw Kreon smiling. She wore a serious expression when she said, "What?"

"Look at my boo being a mommy and shit. That's so sexy." He kissed her on the cheek.

"Shut up," she laughed and playfully punched him. "Help me get this stuff up, so I can take my butt to sleep."

"Alright, slim." He swatted her on her ass just a little too hard, and she jumped up. Afterwards, she punched him and they played Mercy. He picked her up and playfully slammed her down on the couch. They laughed and giggled, continuing to play around.

"Hahahahahahahahahahaha!" Odette tickled him under his armpits as she playfully bit down on his shoulder.

"Hahahahahahhahahahahaha, stop, babe, stop!" Odette cried out jovially, as she was being tickled. She was very ticklish, seeming childlike in her response of the action.

Before Kreon knew it, Marquise was jumping on his back and putting him in a harmless chokehold. He released Odette and rose up, trying to shake the little dude from off his back. While he was doing this, Odette was tickling him as he was laughing aloud.

Marquise jumped down from off Kreon's back and he crumbled to the floor, from the boy's mother tickling him. Mother and son pounced on him, tickling him in his most sensitive areas, making him laugh aloud until he cried. Afterwards, they laid in the middle of the floor, heads lying against each other and breathing hard. There were smiles stretched across their faces.

"This is one for The Book." Odette whipped out her Android cellphone and held it above them. Once she found the shot that she was looking for, she told the boys to say cheese and then snapped several shots. She snapped shots of her and her son kissing Kreon on either cheek, her son and Kreon kissing her, and Marquise and Kreon kissing her. Afterwards, they got ready for bed.

***

Kreon and Odette stood outside of the bathroom door, watching Marquise stand up in a chair before the medicine cabinet's mirror. Toothpaste foam was around his mouth as he brushed his teeth with his Sponge Bob toothbrush, looking like he was wincing. Dots of toothpaste jumped off the boy's grill and clung to the mirror, as he took care of his hygiene. Once he was finished, he sat the toothbrush aside and turned on the faucet. Instantly, water came flowing from out the spout and into the porcelain bowl. He spat into the sink and cupped his hands under the flowing water until they were full, splashing it into his mouth. Once he was done, he shut the water off and jumped down, wiping his mouth with a white towel that was hung on the rack.

He walked over to his mother and said, while smiling, "All fresh and clean."

Odette smiled, thinking how cute her little man looked with his missing front tooth, smiling. She cupped his face with her hands and kissed him on the cheek and the forehead.

"Alright, little man, it's time for bed; let's get chu tucked in." She extended her hand, and he looked between her and Kreon. The youngster looked like he was trying to make a decision.

"Mom, do you mind if Kreon tucks me in?" He looked up at his mother in hope.

A surprised look came over Odette's face and she looked at Kreon like, *it's up to you.*

"Sure, I don't mind. Come on." Kreon started to walk off, but the youngster grabbed his hand. When he did this, Kreon looked from him to his mother; she was smiling with her arms folded across her bosom.

Marquise led Kreon into his bedroom, which was decorated with Sponge Bob merchandise. The little boy's bedroom looked like it was commercial ready. As Marquise jumped into bed and crawled over to the lamp, Kreon stood in the doorway, observing the décor of the bedroom. He could tell that the boy's mother had taken her time fixing the bedroom up in the popular cartoon's theme for her baby boy. He acknowledged that his girlfriend invested a lot of time into her son and his future, and he loved that about her. When the time came, he was sure that she'd make a wonderful mother for their child should they have one, and an even more amazing wife.

Seeing a small light come to life at the corner of his eye, Kreon looked to see that Marquise had just turned on the lamp beside his bed. The youngster then threw the comforter back and laid back upon his pillow, waiting to be tucked in by his mother's boyfriend. Kreon cracked a grin and advanced in the boy's direction. He sat down on the bed and placed the comforter over the boy, tucking him in and handing him a stuffed Sponge Bob. On the side of Kreon, Marquise noticed his mother's silhouette leaned up against the doorway with her arms folded across her bosom still. She tilted her head to the side as she watched her son and her boyfriend attentively.

Kreon placed his hand on Marquise's head and caressed his forehead with his thumb, staring down at his youthful face. The little guy looked sweet and innocent. He had yet to uncover all the ills and horrors that life had to offer. Kreon was happy about that. And should he and the boy's mother remained together, he was going to be sure that he was there every step of the way, to help him get through whatever he faced in the future.

"Alright, my man, this is goodnight." He kissed him on the forehead, knowing that this would be something that he would ask for. He was slowly but surely learning the young man and his mother.

Kreon went to turn out the lamp light, but Marquise stopped him. "Wait."

"What's up?" he asked curiously.

"I overheard you tell my mom that you were sick the other night. Do you have the flu or Chicken Pox?"

Kreon looked between his girlfriend and her son. "I am sick, but not like that. I'm sick up here." He pointed to his temple, meaning his mental state.

"Up there?" Marquise frowned, wondering what he meant by that.

"Yeah, up there." He threw his finger up at his temple again.

"How… how did that happen?"

Kreon looked to Odette and she shrugged, not knowing what to tell him. He figured that she was okay with him telling her son whatever he chose to, so he was going to do just that. See, Kreon was a real ass nigga and he wasn't really up to lying to anyone, not even kids.

Kreon took a deep breath and began, "Growing up… a lotta things happen to me as a kid that I didn't have any control of. There were people that hurt me physically and mentally. I was too young to do anything about it, so I had to take it. Now that I am an adult, I had to somehow manage. I had to somehow cope with all that has occurred."

"Wait…" he sat up in bed, "you said that there were people that hurt chu physically and mentally, right? Well, your mom and dad didn't protect you from them?"

Kreon glanced at Odette again. She was still standing in the doorway in the same pose that she was earlier.

Acknowledging this, he focused his attention back on the young woman's son.

"My mom didn't do much to stop it and, my father, well, the man that I believed was my father. He, uh, he was the person that was hurting me physically and mentally." Kreon told the youth some of the things that not only Khadafi had done to him growing up, but other people as well. He gave him the truth, raw and uncut. After hearing what he had been told, Marquise's eyes pooled with tears and his bottom lip quivered. Before he knew it, the youngster was crying and wiping his tearing eyes with his curled finger.

"What's the matter?" Kreon's forehead crinkled.

Odette came rushing into the bedroom and kneeling beside the bed, beside her son. She took one of his hands into her palm and stared at him, concerned.

"What's wrong, baby?" Worry bled from her eyes.

"I hate them, mommy! I hate them all!" he shouted, emotions causing his voice to crackle.

"Who, baby? Who do you hate?" Odette looked between her son and her man.

"The people that hurt Kreon, mommy. I love him. He's good to us. He's good to me and you," he cried and whimpered.

Abruptly, Marquise threw himself into Kreon and wrapped his arms around his neck, hugging him tightly.

"I'm sorry, Kreon. I'm so, so sorry. You're my best friend, and I won't let anyone else ever, ever, ever hurt chu again. I promise. Me and mommy will protect you." He took his face from the crease of Kreon's neck and looked to the woman that had given birth to him. "Right, mommy? You and me will protect him and make sure no one ever hurts him again." He stared at his mother. There were tears in Odette's eyes and shock was written across her face. She was honestly taken by surprise by her son. He was as much in love with the new man in her life as she was.

"That's right, baby. You and I are gonna make sure nobody ever hurts Kreon again," she assured him, placing her hand on his shoulder.

"You promise?" he asked, cheeks slicked with tears.

"I promise, baby."

With that said, Marquise pulled his mother closer and wrapped his other arm around her neck. He pulled her in snuggly, so that he'd be hugging both her and Kreon at the exact same time. Taking his head from the nape of his mother's neck, he pecked Kreon on the cheek, surprising him. The young nigga blushed and cracked a grin, glassy look coming over his eyes. The love of such a small child fucked him up. It tripped him out that, after all these years, he believed that he wasn't worthy of being loved... here it was two more people besides his uncle that loved him immensely.

Kreon and Odette shut their eyelids at the exact same time, tears sliding down their cheeks continuously. Together, they embraced Marquise in a loving group hug, all three of them crying their eyes out while thinking of all the hurt that Kreon must have experienced in his lifetime.

"We love you, Kreon," Marquise declared.

"I love... I love y'all, too," his voice crackled as he delivered his response and embraced them tighter.

Later that night

Kreon was awakened from his sleep by Odette's neighbor's barking ass dog. He grabbed his .38 and peeked out of the backdoor. He saw their chained-up Pit Bull barking at a homeless man who was rummaging through their black garbage can for recyclables. Seeing this, Kreon decided to give him the few empty plastic bottles that were sitting on the floor beside the trash can on the back porch. Having gathered up all the recyclables and placing them inside of a bag, he walked out into the backyard to give the homeless man the bag of bottles.

"Here you go, my nigga." Kreon passed him the bag of bottles. A smile stretched across the scruffy face of the homeless man, revealing his rotten teeth.

"That's love. Bless you, black man." He took the bag and picked the cross of the crucifix from off his chest, kissing it. When Kreon held out his fist, he dapped him up and tapped his gloved fist to his chest.

"Take it easy out here, my nigga." The young man headed back toward the steps of the back porch.

"Will do." The homeless man tossed the bag into his shopping cart, which was nearly full bags of recyclable goods. He then walked off singing some old song from back in the day, dog still barking at him.

Kreon dipped back inside of the house and shut the door behind him, locking it. He headed into the bathroom, where he pulled out his .38 special and sat it down on the sink. Next, he stepped before the commode and lifted its lid, pulling out his flaccid penis. He then shut his eyelids and tilted his head back, emptied his bladder. Having relieved himself, he shut the commode's lid and flushed the toilet. Stepping before the faucet, he turned on the dial and water came pouring out. Kreon lathered his hands with soap until they were white, and then he proceeded to rinse them off, occasionally glancing up at the mirror at his reflection as he did so. Once he was done, he dashed his hands dry as much as he could and stared at himself in the mirror. Suddenly, he was overwhelmed with great sadness out of the blue. The young man's eyes became pink and glassy, moisture attempting to bleed from them. He clenched his jaws, trying to keep the negative thoughts from forming inside of his mind. But, no matter how much he tried, he wasn't strong enough to keep them at a standstill.

Ain't no bitch gonna won't chu, nigga. You crazy! Hahahahahahahaha!

Wait 'til she finds out just how fucked up you are, dawg! You gone send that lil' bitch runnin'.

"Shut up, shut up, shut up!" Kreon squeezed his eyelids shut and pounded his temples with his fists. Tear coated his cheeks and spittle dashed the medicine cabinet's mirror. "You don't know shit, you bitch ass nigga; I'm the man! I'm the mothafuckin' man! You hear me, pussy?" He jabbed his finger at his reflection. "I made it through all of that shit that came at me in life, I beat that shit! Me, and I'ma beat cho ass too."

I hear you, playa; maybe you will beat me. But, tell me this though, who's gonna love you? Huh? Who's gonna love your sick ass, nigga? You're fat, ugly, stupid, and crazy as a shit-house rat! Yo' pops didn't want chu, ya mom's let em beat cho ass, ya g-pops dead, and all yo' homies turned they backs on you. Why is it that you can't seem to see that no one loves you, Kreon? Huh? Shit, nigga, I'm you and I don't even love you!

"O loves me, though. I can feel it when she looks at me!"

You think so? What about the others you told yo' secret too, huh? Them bitches bounced like you had the Ebola virus, nigga. I'm tellin' you, big boy. The moment you tell homegirl what's up, her ass gone take off like a 747. Do yo' self a favor here, my nigga... pick up your 30 and stick it into yo' grill.

"No! Noo! I won't!" he spat, struggling to get a grip on himself. The tears were flowing freely down his face and snot oozed out of his right nostril. His entire form appeared to be trembling as he continued to struggle with what his mind urged him to do, gritting his teeth.

Hesitantly, Kreon's hand slowly moved towards .38 on the sink. He picked it up and brought it towards his lips, opening his mouth.

There we go, champ. Now, pull that there trigga back and send us off to a place where it's always sunny and the birds are chirping.

Kreon shut his eyelids tight and bit down on the cold, blue steel barrel inside of his grill. His finger slowly curled around the trigger of the pistol, gently pulling it back. Kreon swallowed the lump of nervousness in his throat and his body shuddered, but he knew he had to push himself into what his mind was tricking him into believing what needed to be done.

Knock! Knock! Knock!

"Kreon, come out. I gotta pee, babe!" Odette spoke groggily and wiped the corner of her eye with her knuckle, tapping her foot impatiently; she was definitely in a tight to pee.

Kreon's head snapped to the door and he took the revolver out of his mouth, barrel glistening from his saliva. Swallowing his spit and tasting the weapon's steel, he replied. "I'ma... I'ma be out in a minute, baby," his voice crackled under his raw emotion.

Odette frowned up, hearing how he sounded. She could tell something was troubling him, and he was trying to mask it. "Bae, are you okay?"

Kreon's head shuddered and tears dripped from his eyes. His shaking hand brought his revolver to his temple; he squeezed his eyelids shut. Snot oozed out of both of his nostrils. He was trying his hardest to fight back those evil thoughts in his head, but life had been so mothafucking cruel to him. For once, he wanted a moment's peace. For once, he wanted to rest without being awakened out of his sleep by his nightmares. *Was that too much to ask for?*

Do it. Hurry up! Hurry up before she busts in here and tries to stop you!

She started pounding on the door with her fist. "Kreon, what's going on?"

"I'm tired, baby. I'm so tired," he sobbed, big teardrops splashing on the tiled floor and his flat foot.

"Kreon, what are you talking about? What are you tired of?"

"Living…"

She gasped and her eyes widened, heart quickening in her chest.

"No, baby, no! Oh, God! Don't do this to me! I love you, Kreon! I love you so much!" *Boom! Boom! Boom! Boom!* Her fist rapidly pounded on the door. "We can beat this, we can beat this together!" she cried, tears cascading down her face while her eyes turned pink. Her heart was beating madly, like it was trying to leap through her chest.

"No, no, no, no." He shook his head and the tears continued to fall. He pressed the .38 further into his temple. "I'm tired! I'm tired of going through this shit, man!" He pounded his large fist on the edge of the sink.

"Don't do nothing, don't chu do nothing, you hear me?" She threw her short body into the door, trying to break it open. "You owe me, remember? You owe me a happily ever after."

"Somebody else can give it to you!"

"Nooooooo!" she screamed, veins rolling up her temples and neck. "You give it to me! I want it with you! I want you to be my husband; I want to bear your first child! I want to wake up in the morning and roll over to your handsome face! Don't do this to me, don't do this to us!" She stepped back and started kicking the door at its lock. *Boom! Boom! Boom!* It came flying open, sending splinters flying everywhere. She tackled her lover just as he pulled the trigger of his revolver, fire spitting from the weapon's barrel. The bullet it disengaged went wild and struck the ceiling, causing debris to fall.

Odette straddled Kreon, both crying. She smacked him across the face repeatedly. "What were you doing? What the fuck were you doing? Huh? You were just going to leave me? Leave us? Me and Marquise?" *Smack! Smack! Smack!* Her hands came across his face viciously. She shuddered and her tears fell faster. Some of them hit his face. He started coming off his suicide high, seeing how his decision had affected her. Suddenly, she stopped hitting him and collapsed on top of him. Her body shook violently as she laid on top of him, crying her eyes out. Slowly, his arms wrapped around her and he rubbed her back soothingly.

"Don't leave me, babe. Don't ever leave me. I love you! I love you so fucking much!" she sobbed and shook some more. She truly was terrified of losing him. For as fucked up as he was, she knew that the love he had for her was genuine.

"I love you, too."

"Well, promise me then, promise me that you'll never leave me." She looked up at him.

"I promise. I'm sorry, Slim." His eyes looked down at her.

She laid her head back against his chest and said, "Now hold me, hold me tight."

He did just that and, eventually, they fell asleep together, on the bathroom floor.

That morning

Odette stood at the stove, repeatedly wiping her tearing eyes as she cooked breakfast. She couldn't get over the fact that Kreon had tried to bring his life to an end. For the life of her, she couldn't understand why he wanted to commit suicide. She tried getting him to open up to her, but he brushed her off. When they'd awakened on the bathroom floor, she went on to start cooking, while he went on about the task of taking care of his hygiene.

Odette cut the fire off her skillet of eggs and finished whipping them until they had formed to her liking. Afterwards, she turned off the stove and pulled out a pan of biscuits, placing them on top of the stove. She heard Kreon rummaging inside of the refrigerator when she was placing the crisp bacon onto a plate covered by a folded bed of paper towels.

"Mar Mar, come eat!" Odette called out to her son. All she and Kreon could hear were a pair of feet running through the house, the sound growing louder and louder until the little guy arrived inside of the kitchen.

Odette went onto to make their plates while Kreon poured up three glasses of orange juice; one for him, her, and little man. There was silence among the couple, being that they were trying to avoid discussing his suicide attempt. Odette sat her son and her man's plates down before them, then sat down at the opposite end of the table. They quietly ate their breakfast, with Marquise asking the occasional question. Besides that, the only reoccurring sound was their forks hitting their dishes and the munching of their food.

"Bae!" Odette called out to him. Suddenly, Kreon stopped his fork of eggs at his lips, jaws swollen with food. His eyes stared up at her, hoping that she didn't ask him again about his wanting to kill himself. "Pass me the salt, please."

He nodded yes and passed her the item that she desired. They went on eating. Marquise hurriedly finished his meal, so he could play his PlayStation. His mother chuckled at him and called him a game freak, but went on to oblige him when he asked to be excused. Again, his feet could be heard running through the house. This time, the sound got softer and softer until it was gone.

Odette laid down her fork and lifted her glass, holding it at her lips. "Soooo, uh, how is your mother doing?"

Again, Kreon stopped his fork at his mouth, jaws full like he was thinking about something. He munched and swallowed his food before speaking again.

"Fuck my momma!" he spat like he had a nasty taste in his mouth.

Odette's face balled up and she said, "Wow! Baby, that's your mother."

He then went back to eating until he'd cleaned his plate. Afterwards, he sat his fork down on his plate and wiped his mouth with a napkin.

"I know that. Listen, I love my mom's to death. She's been there for me, but not when I needed her most. So, fuck that bitch, I'm not sure if I care if she dies."

Odette frowned and angled her head. "Watch yo' mouth now! I know you may have resentment toward her, but I know you didn't mean what chu just said."

Balling up the napkin, Kreon leaned back in his chair and burped with his fist to his mouth. "Are you sure about that?" He looked her dead in her eyes, speaking with a truthful tongue. She matched his gaze and saw through his eyes, that he meant what he said.

"Why do you act so heartless, so cold?" Her brows furrowed and her eyes narrowed, looking at him like he was illegible writing that she was trying to read on paper. He could be the sweetest person in the world at times and others, well, he could be something else altogether.

By this time, Kreon was rinsing off his plate. When she stated this, he whipped around and said, "Who said it's an act?"

"I know you aren't completely without feelings," she said, so sure of herself. "I know how lovey dovey you are with me and I see how you treat my son."

"What is this all about?"

"You acting like you don't give a fuck about nothing or no one."

He twisted his lips and raised an eyebrow saying, "I don't."

She coiled her neck, looking at him like *what?*

"You must think I'm bullshittin'. I don't give a fuck about nothing or no one." He looked her square in the eyes.

"What happened to you? What happened to you to make you how you are? I know there's gotta be something.

"You gotta give me something, bae. I'm in love witchu, but I hardly know anything about chu." She cried, hot tears flooding her cheeks. While she was talking, his back was to her, still washing the dishes. "I've told you things about me."

He angrily smacked the plate he'd just rinsed off into the dish rack, turned off the faucet, and turned around to her.

"The mood swings, the sarcasm, the rages... something tells me that there's a story behind all of it. And if you're willing to tell me, then I'm willing to listen." She stared at him as she waited for his response.

"I told you in the beginnin' that I don't talk about myself and you said you wouldn't pry," He mad dogged her, wiping his hands dry with a towel and tossed it over his shoulder.

"That was before."

"Before what?"

"Before I fell in love."

He chuckled, looked away, and turned his back to her, shaking his head. She felt stupid now. She had fallen for him but he hadn't for her, or at least he was portraying not to have.

"You in love with me, O?" His face held an amused expression.

"Yes, very much so, and thank you for making me feel stupid." She wiped the wetness from her face.

"Like you needed my help with that," he remarked, opening the refrigerator and taking out a pitcher of ice tea. What he said made her brows furrow. "Fuck you fall in love with a nigga in two weeks?" He shook his head, pitifully. She felt herself shrinking right there on the spot. Although she had told him that she loved him in such a short time, she couldn't help it. That's truly how she felt.

"Excuse me. I was under the impression that you felt the same." She folded her arms across her chest, switching her weight to her other foot.

"I do love you, but I know everything there is to know about you. Shit, you said it yourself, sweetheart; you hardly know anything about me, yet you're in love. Where they do that at?"

"Damn, that was cold, real cold." She felt that dagger straight through the heart; the tears came flying down her face, unevenly. She tried her best to hold them back, but that last one stung.

"I'm only speakin' the truth, love."

She swiped away the fresh tears, tapping her foot heatedly. She was mad and hurt. "You know what, Kreon? I'm starting to believe that what we have going isn't that serious for you, that you've been playing with my emotions this entire time. So, I'm going to ask you something, and I want you to tell me the true, okay?" He nodded. "Did you ever really love me?"

"I fucks witchu, O, you cool people, but…" He slight grinned and shrugged. Although he saw her tears, he didn't give a fuck about them. "I'm just not that into you."

"Wow." She wiped away more of her tears. "What're we doing here then, Kreon?" She opened her arms.

"We talkin'."

"You know what the fuck I mean!" she spat back, agitated.

"I do?" He raised his eyebrows.

"Do you even care about me?"

"I told you that you cool people," he said, as if he was getting annoyed by her.

"Unh unh, this is some bullshit." She closed the distance between them. "You look me in my eyes and tell me that I mean nothing to you. That the night we met at The Bar Fly, you didn't feel the chemistry between us." He rolled his eyes and blew hot air, not really trying to get all in his feelings and shit. "If you can tell me that…" her voice crackled under her raw emotions and she wiped the tears that threatened to fall. Clearing her throat, she pressed on. "If you can tell me that, then I want you to walk out of that door," she pointed to the front door without taking her eyes off him, "and never turn back. You'll never have to worry about seeing me or my son again."

Her voice trailed off; she could feel it in her throat that she was about to start bawling, but she had a feeling that her grieving was fueling his nonchalant attitude and she didn't want to give him the satisfaction.

"Is that what chu want?" he scowled; they were standing face to face. They were so close they could feel one another's breaths on their faces.

"I want the truth." She stared that nigga square in his eyes.

He cleared his throat with a fist to his mouth. Looking her square in her face, he said, "You don't mean anything to me. In fact, I'll forget about chu just as soon as I'm outta that door. That's the truth for yo' mothafuckin' ass, but I see now that you can't handle it."

Her face twisted and hot tears coated her cheeks. Veins rolled up her neck and forehead, and she turned rose red in the face. She bit down on her bottom lip as her chest rose and fell rapidly, like her heart was trying desperately to punch its way out of her body.

"Fuck you finna do? Cry some more?"

"You fucking bastard!"

Smack!

His head snapped to the left and he slowly turned back around to her. She just knew that he was about to beat her ass, but he didn't.

"I hope that made you feel betta." He licked his bleeding lip.

She mad dogged him for a time, wanting to fight him, although she knew that she couldn't win against him. The odds were against her. She figured that it was best that she just left things be and let him be on his way. She made up her mind that she wasn't going to cry any more in front of him though. Nah, she'd wait until he was gone before she broke down.

"Let me get my shit, so I can go."

Kreon walked passed Odette and headed for her bedroom to get all his shit. Her heart shattered into one million pieces and her body trembled violently. Water built up in her eyes and obscured her vision. Shutting her eyelids, she summoned up the strength to hold all her emotions back until he was finally out of the door.

"Come lock this door," Kreon said to her, adjusting his jacket as he headed for the front door. "I'm getting the fuck outta here."

Odette followed Kreon to the door and opened it for him, stepping aside. He stood where he was, staring her in the eyes. It was at that moment that he felt like the world's biggest piece of shit for how he had treated her. He didn't want to go the remainder of his life without seeing her, holding her, talking to her... making love to her. A life without Odette was something he didn't even want to imagine, which was funny considering all the shit that he was just talking. He found himself on the verge of an anxiety attack, panic running rapid throughout his mind. His knees felt weak and he thought that they were going to buckle. But, he had to stay strong; he couldn't let her see that their breaking up was scaring the hell out of him.

"So, you just gone leave me?" Kreon's eyes became moist. He could feel himself panicking and reverting to a child, a child that his father didn't want or love. A child that got little to no affection of time from his mother; that little boy that had been bullied, abused, deprived, and made to feel like he didn't matter in the world. The last thing he wanted was to be abandoned, to be thrown away like trash. He couldn't bear it. He couldn't take it. Although he was the one that initiated the idea, the thought of it made his stomach turn and his chest tighten.

"Leave you, Kreon? Really? You're the one leaving me," she told him. "From your actions, this is obviously how you wanted it, so this is goodbye. Have a nice life."

With that said, Kreon felt extremely faint and weak. He blinked his eyelids rapidly and grabbed the doorway, so he wouldn't fall.

"Haa! Wheeze! Haa! Wheeze! Haa!" He grabbed at his shirt and ruffled it, staring at her like he was about to pass out.

"Oh, my God, bae; are you alright?" Odette asked concerned, putting her arms around his waist.

"Yeah… yeah." He nodded. "I just… I just don't want to lose you, babe."

"What?" Her brows furrowed. She looked at him like he was crazy. "After all of that stuff you were saying back inside of the kitchen? You said that…"

Kreon waved her off and said, "I was just talkin' outta my ass, O. A nigga love you, girl. A nigga really, really love you. I'd be sick without you, straight up. You know that I didn't mean that. I'm crazy about chu, O."

"If you mean what you're saying and you truly do love me. Then, you're gonna start having to act like it, Kreon. Okay?" He nodded yes, and she wiped her tears away with the back of her fist. "Cause I deserve better than this, I'm a good person." Her voice cracked from his hurting her feelings. She thought she could hold it together, but she was unraveling at the seams.

"I'm sorry, babe. I fucked up." He hugged her tightly. She stared over her shoulder, rubbing his hand up and down his back while tears slid down her cheeks.

"Why though, bae? Why did you say though things to me? Don't I treat you good? Don't I make you feel special?"

"Yeah." He pulled back and looked at her.

"Then, why did you say those things to me?" she inquired, looking into his eyes as he wiped the wetness from her cheeks with the lower half of his shirt.

"Cause I hate you."

"What?" Lines went across her forehead and she angled her head. "I didn't do anything to you. All I did was love you, Kreon. And all I ever wanted was for you to love me back." She cried and sniffled. All her life, she had been searching for the love of her father in every man that she dated. She desperately wanted someone to love and protect her, just like her old man was supposed to.

While she needed love, Kreon learned to survive without it. The young man felt that such an emotion made one weak, and he never wanted to be weak for anyone. Because to be vulnerable meant the possibility that he could become a victim. He'd be damned if he allowed that to happen as an adult, when he'd been a victim all his childhood. Nuh unh, fuck that.

"When I met chu, I was ready to die, but chu made me wanna live again." He blinked back tears. Men were supposed to be as solid as a rock. Big, tough, emotionless, this was how the men in his family were. This was how society said he was supposed to be. To act in any other way would mean that you were feminine, a broad, for lack of better words… a bitch.

Odette shut the door closed. "How did I make you wanna live again?"

Kreon didn't utter a word; he just stared ahead at something only he could see. He looked like he was in a trance or watching a movie that he could only see.

"Kreon! Kreon! Kreon," Odette called after him, sounding like she was being left down in a tunnel. She grabbed him by the front of his shirt and shook him, causing his head to bob back and forth. Her efforts were fruitless though, because he was staring in one of the scenes of the movie that was his life.

Flashback

Khadafi had fallen victim to smoking crack. Once he spent all his money and couldn't get any more from Ella to support his habit, he sold the Rolex watch that she'd bought him for his birthday. Knowing that Ella would be devastated and heartbroken when she found out what he'd done, he placed the blame on Kreon, telling her that he'd stolen it and pawned it and that's how he was able to buy the new Jordans.

The only problem was, Ella knew that he'd sold the watch to a hustler for crack. She found out through one of her friends, whose man was a drug dealer from around the way. He'd come home the day prior, rocking the same watch she'd given Khadafi for his birthday. Ella wasn't sure that it was her man's at first but, once she read the inscription on the back of the watch's face, To Big Daddy from Big Momma, she knew without a shadow of a doubt that the watch belonged to him. When Ella brought this up to Khadafi, they got into a big argument that drew Kreon from his bedroom to see what the fuck was going on. When he'd made it inside of his parent's bedroom, the verbal altercation was at its all-time high.

"You gone and get da fuck up from outta here, bitch!" Khadafi's nostrils flared as he pointed to the bedroom door. He was glaring at Ella and a fifteen-year-old, Kreon.

"Nigga, did you just call my momma a bitch?" Young Kreon huffed and puffed, his eyebrows arched while taking on a menacing appearance. He charged after his father. His mother tried to grab his arm and stop him, but it was already too late; the Pit Bull was off its leash.

Brackk! Bwap!

Khadafi staggered backwards and hit the floor, bleeding from his bottom lip. He blinked his eyelids rapidly, trying to get a hold on where he was. He tried to pull himself up by grabbing a hold of the bed; his son came up behind him, dropping them thangs on his head. The nigga managed to scramble upon his feet and dash on the side of the mattress. Lifting it up while still getting punched in his exposed face, he grabbed the black, scarred .38 Bull Dog. Gripping it with both hands, he swung the banged-up piece around. Kreon froze where he was, but he didn't show any signs of fear. Nah, he just waited to see what was going to happen next. It appeared as if his father's finger was moving in slow motion as it curled around the trigger and the chamber of the pistol spun. The young man's mother came up from behind him, screaming something that was inaudible to him, being that he and his old man only existed in his world.

The chamber of the pistol made a complete turn and a metal click sound. The sound of the atmosphere came flooding back to Kreon, and reality was restored. His eyes settled on the chamber of the weapon; he saw that it wasn't fully loaded. This angered the youngster and he raged forth, pummeling his father. His head flew from left to right as the solid blows met with his head and face. The older man seemed to be losing consciousness as his attacker was pulled off him by his mother.

"You bitch ass nigga, don't chu ever disrespect my momma!" Spittle flew off Kreon's lips as his mother held him back from Khadafi, desperately trying to keep him at bay.

"Kreon, calm down, calm yo ass down!" she urged him, cupping her hands around his face. She stared into his eyes. They were glassy and his nostrils were pulsating. His chest pumped up and down like a cannon was erupting inside of it. "Are you, alright? Are you, okay?"

"I'm fine, Ma."

"Let me see yo' hands." She took his hands into her own and studied them. They were busted up and bleeding, in the beginning stages of swelling. Her face balled up seeing how pained they looked, but her son didn't seem to be the least bit fazed by his injuries.

A sudden rush of air from behind mother and son stole their attention. Their heads snapped around and they found Khadafi hustling down the steps with his pistol. They figured that he was going to stash it somewhere, worrying that Ella was going to call the police on him.

"Come on, we gotta catch up with yo' father." Ella grabbed Kreon by his wrist and hurried down the staircase.

Ella prowled the streets until the wee hours of the morning, looking for Khadafi. She found him inside of a trap house intoxicated, having sold his .38 for some crack. When he came to, he pleaded for her forgiveness and she took him back with opened arms. Their relationship finally ended once Kreon shot at him for beating on his mother. As the man hauled ass down the street, his son promised him that, if he ever returned, he'd blow his brains out.

Present

"Kreon! Kreeoon! Kreeeooon!" Odette shook him as hard as she could. Finally, he squeezed his eyelids shut and then peeled them apart, looking her directly in her eyes.

"Yeah."

Lines deepened her forehead as she stared up at him, probing his eyes. "Where… where were you just now?" He didn't say anything. He just continued to stare into her eyes. That's when she cupped her hands around his face and stared deep into his eyes. "Oh, my goodness, your eyes… they're… they're so lifeless, soulless even. All I see is sadness in them, a great, great sadness."

Kreon stood there emotionless and expressionless. He was like a robot in that moment. There weren't any signs of what he was feeling or thinking. It was like this for him a lot of times. It was one of the symptoms of his mental illness.

Kreon grasped her wrists and took them from off his face. He took a deep breath and turned his glassy eyes on to her. "Can you see why I say I'm not normal now? Why I feel like I'm subhuman? A demon or monster doesn't have a soul. But men… all men have them, except for me."

When he said this, Odette hugged him tightly. He stared at nothing over her shoulder as he became teary eyed. Odette kissed him on the cheek and wiped the wetness from the corner of his eyes away with her thumbs. Seeing his eyes dart to the left, she turned around and found Marquise standing in the doorway. A worried expression was on his face as he looked from his mother to her boyfriend, wondering what was going on between them.

"Mar Mar, come here sweetie." Odette motioned her son over and he came running, bare feet smacking down on the linoleum. She kneeled to her son and told him. "Is Kreon your friend?" He nodded yes. "Do you love him?" He nodded yes again. "Well, tell him; give him a hug and tell him that you love him."

Odette looked to her man and nudged him. This was his signal to kneel to her baby boy, and he did. Marquise approached his best friend and looked him square in the eyes. "I love you, Kreon," He kissed him on the cheek and embraced him lovingly.

"I love you too, lil' dude." He embraced him back and lifted him up. When he turned to his lady, he had tears sliding down his cheeks. He motioned her over to him and she came, forming a group hug. Odette and Marquise squeezed the man in their lives tightly. At that moment, he'd gotten all the love that he'd never received in all his 27 years of living. This overwhelmed him and he broke down, silently sobbing and body shaking. More tears came bursting through his shut eyelids, his bottom lip shivered. His loved ones embraced him that much more and he did the same.

CHAPTER SEVEN
That night

Jaekwon stood at the kitchen counter making himself a bologna sandwich, his gun lying beside all the items he needed to make it. The only sound inside of his studio apartment was the tv in the front room, which Paw Patrol was on. The television flashed a blue light on the bed that his toddler laid asleep on, pacifier in his mouth. He was a golden brown little fella, with a dimpled chin and cornrows. Jaekwon was taking care of him, while his baby momma went to enjoy herself on a girls' night out. Usually, he bitched and complained about having to watch their child but, with God only knew how many niggaz looking to kill him, he didn't mind kicking it at home to try to figure out his next move.

Knocks at the door instantly caused Jaekwon to stiffen, heart booming inside of his chest. Turning his head over his shoulder, he sucked the Miracle Whip residue from off his fingers and listened for the knocking that had recently stopped. It started up again and he wiped his hands off on a towel lying on the counter. Next, he picked up his ratchet and crept to the door, looking through the peep in the door. His heart's rapid beating slowed a bit, once he saw that it was his cousin. He tucked his banger on his waistline, unchaining and unlocking his door. When he pulled it open, he exchanged pleasantries with Kreon and allowed him inside.

"Sup, fool? You were in the hood or something?" he asked, chaining and locking the door back.

"Yeah, man, thought I'd see what's up with my relative."

"That's what's up." He nodded, genuinely happy to see his first cousin. They hadn't kicked it like that since they were 13-years-old, running the streets together. They were as good as blood brothers but, nowadays, they weren't as tight they used to be. But, things changed once Jaekwon started gang banging. He tried to get Kreon to join him, but he declined, reasoning that them niggaz didn't love them like they claim they did. Besides, the nigga wasn't a follower. He'd decided to do his own thing.

"My lil' relative knocked out," Kreon said, seeing Jaekwon's son asleep on the bed. Jaekwon had just disappeared inside of the kitchen, "Where yo' B.M.?"

"She out at the club with Meeka and the rest of them ol' chicken head hoes."

"Oh." Kreon nodded, checking the rest of the unit to make sure no one else was present to witness him about to do what he had planned. "Just you and lil' dude here, huh?"

"Yeahhhh."

While Jaekwon went about the task of making his sandwich with his back to Kreon, he was approaching the kitchen while drawing his blue steel .38. After peeking over at the bed and seeing his baby cousin asleep sucking his bottle and playing in his curly hair, he twisted his face into a scowl and moved to do the evil deed that his mind had manifested. Gun at his side, he approached the kitchen's doorway, watching his prey and listening to him rap the lyrics to Biggie Smalls' *You're Nobody 'Til Somebody Kills You.*

"Yo' you wanna sandwich, Blood?" Jaekwon asked as he spread Miracle Whip on a slice of bread. Once he was done, he sucked the residue from off his thumb and began with the other.

"Yeah, hook me up, Reli," Kreon replied with his head tilted down and his eyes glaring up at his intended victim. His plan was to knock the yoke out of his egg and dip off. As his cousin began fixing the second sandwich, Kreon lifted his banger and pointed it at the back of his head. His heart thundered inside of his chest; it was all he could hear besides the butter knife clinking against the jar of Miracle Whip as his cousin made the sandwich.

Kreon shut his eyelids briefly and took a deep breath, his shoulders dropping. He went to pull the trigger when he saw a shadow on the floor behind him. Dropping the hand holding the revolver to his side, he snapped around and found Jaekwon's son. The boy was standing there with a curious expression across his face. Seeing this, he tucked his weapon at the small of his back and scooped little dude up. He smiled and bounced his little cousin on his arm, cracking a slight smile on his lips. A crooked line formed on Jaekwon's forehead and he turned around, wondering what was going on. When he saw his cousin holding his son, he grinned.

"Lil' nigga look just like me, huh?" He threw his head back.

"Yeahhh, he do." Kreon observed his younger relative's face, seeing that he did have an uncanny resemblance to his father. He couldn't help thinking that if his dad was a rat, then he was possibly holding a mouse in his arms.

Kreon passed his little relative to his father while saying, "Yo, I'ma get up on outta here, my nigga. I gotta couple moves I gotta make."

"Alright, Reli, peace out." He extended his hand. Kreon looked at his open palm and allowed it to linger for a time, before shaking it with his left hand. Jaekwon frowned when he saw this, but shook the meaning behind it out of his head. Surely, his people hadn't heard about him running his mouth behind closed doors. Although he was a street nigga, he was still naïve about how the system worked. There was no such thing as a confidential informant. Eventually, whatever you told the police would come to the light for everyone to know.

When Kreon turned around to head out of the door, he noticed that heat at the back of him. An even deeper line formed on his forehead but, again, he shook the thought from his head that something was up.

"Yo, Reli!" Kreon turned around and threw his head back like *what's up?* "Tuck yo' shit up, my nigga. You know The Ones are hotta den fish grease out this way."

"Ooooh, G lookin'." Kreon put his banger up and went on about his business.

***

Kreon looked around cautiously before whipping out his .38 and opening the driver's door of his Pontiac. He slid in behind the wheel of his Pontiac and slammed the door shut behind him. He tucked his revolver underneath the driver's seat and laid back against the headrest, staring up at the ceiling.

"You stupid, stupid, stupid mothafucka..." Kreon said to no one in particular, voice slowly rising in octaves. "You just couldn't keep yo' goddamn mouth shut, huh? You just fuckin' couldn't!" He spoke of Jaekwon's being a confidential informant, scowling and gritting his teeth. Overwhelmed with rage, he turned his anger on the ceiling, punching it with all his might. His fists slamming into it back to back, attacking it until he grew exhausted. He stopped abruptly, letting his hands fall at his sides. His forehead and neck were shiny from perspiration and his nostrils were flaring from breathing so hard. His chest rose and fell rapidly as he ran his hand down his face, licking his lips. Tears cascaded down his cheeks, feeling hurt and betrayed from what his relative had done. He hated him for putting him in a position where he'd have to kill him, but understood that he had to do what had to be done.

"Cousin or no cousin, I shoulda just off'd his ass, tall skinny fuckin' bastard! I shoulda just blew his head off right there in front of his son. He's a rat and his son's a mouse; lil' nigga probably grow up to be just like his ass. Fuck it, it ain't too late!" He wiped his tearing eye with the back of his fist and reached underneath the seat, pulling out his blue steel. He opened the driver's door and was about to hop out but stopped himself short. Slowly, he slammed the door shut and slid his revolver back underneath the seat.

"Sheiiit." He bowed his head and shook it, massaging the bridge of his nose. "Fuck is I'm talkin' about? I can't do no shit like that. I'm betta than that, they family." He leaned his head back against the headrest, staring wide-eyed at the ceiling. He took one deep breath, expelling his frustration. "He a snitch, but I love that nigga; we grew up together. Niggaz, we're like brothas…" Kreon sat up in his seat and stuck his key into the ignition, turning it. The vehicle roared to life and he cracked the window. "I'ma let this nigga breathe, karma will catch up to 'em… bitch ass nigga." He glanced in the side view mirror. When he didn't see any cars coming, he pulled out into the residential street and drove off down the block.

A few nights later

Kreon lie in bed in the dark, staring up at the ceiling with his hands clasped behind his head. Every time his future came to mind, all he saw was a blank canvass. Sure, there were things that he wanted to do, but he didn't see them happening. He reasoned that, if he didn't see his future happening, he wasn't going to be alive to see one. Thinking this, he took a deep breath and blew hot air. His life was frustrating as fuck. He didn't know whether he was coming or going.

The ringing and vibrating of his cellular brought Kreon's attention around to the side of the bed. Rolling over, he picked up the cellphone that was lying on the floor. A line creased his forehead when he saw his cousin, Jaekwon's, name and number on the screen. It was one o'clock in the morning, so he figured that someone had either died or had gotten locked up; either way, he had to answer to see what was up.

Kreon adjusted himself in bed and answered his cellular, placing it to his ear, "Sup, nigga?"

"I need you to come get me," Jaekwon whispered, sounding scared as a mothafucka.

Kreon sat up in bed. "Fuck is going on?"

"Niggaz is tryna take me out, Blood."

Why am I not surprised, old tellin' ass nigga? Kreon thought, shaking his head disappointedly.

"Niggaz tryna take you out for what? Fuck you at?"

Jaekwon told him exactly where he was and what had occurred. He had come out of the China Town Express over on Western Avenue and some niggaz in a royal-blue Honda Civic had tried to lay him down. He got busy with his tool and took out the shooter, managing to escape with his life, but he was bleeding at the shoulder. He'd taken a hot one there. Now, he was over his side chick's house, who just so happened to be an LVN, licensed vocational nurse, and she was cleaning and dressing his wound for him at the moment. He'd left his car at the parking lot inside of the shopping center when the firefight had started and little momma used public transportation, so there wasn't any way that he could leave. His face was on several news channels from the incident, so he didn't want to risk being caught while out on foot.

Initially, he thought that Omar had found out about him snitching and sent some niggaz to peel his cap but, once he found out who the fool was that he killed through news broadcasts, he knew that *that* most definitely wasn't the case.

Homeboy that had tried to knock off his onion was a cat by the name of Set Trip. He was the baby daddy of this broad that he was banging. They'd bumped heads once at the Slauson Swapmeet over dude's baby's momma, and he swore to kill him the next time he saw him. That night, his chipped tooth ass tried to make good on that threat, but he fucked around and got killed. With his death came the manhunt for Jaekwon. Now, it would be in the young nigga'z best interest to get whatever cash he could get his hands on and get the fuck out of Killa Cali, or face going to trial for murder.

Jaekwon was backed up in a corner. Omar wasn't answering his phone, but he was confident that Kreon would pick up his jack. If there was anyone that he could count on to have his back, it was his cousin. He knew there wasn't a nigga standing on two legs that his relative was afraid of and, if it came down to it, he'd bust his gun for him.

"Where you want me to take you?" Kreon asked, cradling the cell to his ear. He was leaning over and tying up his Chuck Taylor Converses. Afterwards, he reached underneath his pillow and grabbed his revolver, stashing it at the back of his Dickies.

"Greyhound, bro, I'ma duck off in Arkansas with my pop's family. Already let 'em know that a nigga was comin'."

"Alright, cool. I'll be there in like fifteen or twenty minutes."

"Fa sho'. I love you, bro."

There was silence for a time as Kreon cupped his hand around a Black & Mild and sparked it up, blowing out smoke.

"I love you too, my nigga." He disconnected the call and slipped the device inside of his pocket. Stepping to the door, he thought he heard someone sniffling and crying. This caused his forehead to deepen with crevasses. He looked to his mother's bedroom. Taking the thin cigar from out of his mouth, he blew smoke and made a beeline for her domain. He knocked on her door and called her name, but he didn't receive an answer. Next, he turned the knob and entered, crossing the threshold. He found her bundled up with her back to the door. He called her name again as he advanced in her direction, but she didn't reply. Still at her back, he crawled into bed and kissed her on the side of her head.

Ella's face was stained white with dried tears. As soon as she heard the bedroom door click shut, her glassy, red webbed eyes stretched open. Her chest rose and fell as she breathed softly. She waited a while longer before sitting up in bed and preparing to make her departure, not only from the apartment but from her son's life.

***

Kreon backed his Pontiac up into Jaekwon's side chick's driveway and popped the trunk. His cousin snuck out from the backdoor of the house and cautiously came down the driveway, head on a swivel. He dapped up his relative and climbed inside of the trunk, allowing Kreon to slam it shut. Having slammed the trunk closed, Kreon made his way around to the driver side and hopped in behind the wheel. Resurrecting the Grand Am, he drove off while kicking himself in the ass for putting his neck on the line for his punk ass cousin.

"I can't believe I'm helpin' this nigga after he done shitted on me and Unc." Kreon shook his head, thinking about how his cousin had dropped a dime on him and Omar. "Bitch ass nigga." Frustrated, he ran his hand down his face and blew hot air, conflicted. "He's family though, fuuuuck!"

He slammed his fist down on the steering wheel, rattling it. Afterwards, he stuck what was left of the Black & Mild in between his lips, looking back and forth between the road ahead while fishing around inside of the change tray for his Bic lighter. Gripping the steering wheel with one hand, he looked back and forth between the windshield and his cigar as he lit it with the other, its golden orange licking at the tip of it. The street lights flickered on and off his face with each of the illuminating light posts that he passed under, the sounds of cars whipping past him in traffic. Having successfully lit the Black, he tossed the lighter back inside of the tray and took big puffs, narrowing his eyelids. Smoke wafted around him and he fanned it away with his hand. Once it drove him to coughing, he cracked the window to give himself a little air.

Kreon popped in Dr. Dre's *Chronic 2001* and went through the tracks until he found the one that he was looking for. A moment later, *Bitch Nigga* came pumping from the speakers. He nodded his head to it and glanced over his shoulder, twisting the dial. "This next joint is for you, Reli."

He was spitting the lyrics to Snoop's verse when his cellular rang. Seeing the light blue illumination from its screen from his right where it was lying in the passenger seat, he picked it up and looked at the display. The caller identification said unknown, which caused his brows to furrow. Normally, he didn't even fuck with blocked numbers, let alone unknown ones, but his curiosity got the best of him. He had to see who it was.

"What's up with it?" he spoke into the device. As he listened to the caller, his brows furrowed further and further. "That was me. You were there? I know, I know. Shits fucked up, but what a nigga 'pose to do though." He shook his head as he continued to listen to the caller. His eyes looked to the rearview mirror and he adjusted it, seeing a pair of headlights flashing twice.

"You see those lights flashing?" the caller asked.

"Yeah, I see 'em."

"That's me. Gon' pull over."

"Man, I-"

"I got chu faded, homeboy. Pull over to the side of the road, dawg, alright?"

Kreon took a deep breath, closing his eyelids for a moment as he contemplated. Once he peeled them back open, he had his mind made up. His eyes were glassy though. He was about to deliver his answer but, when he went to speak, he heard his voice about to crack under his emotions, so he cleared his throat.

"Alright," He disconnected the call and stashed the cellular inside of his hoodie. He glanced to his right and then pulled his car over like he was instructed to do. Moments later, a silver Nissan Sentra pulled up behind him. He could tell by the plates that it was a rental. Mashing out his Black, he jumped out of his whip at the exact same time the driver of the Nissan was hopping out of his. The two of them approached one another, the driver's facial features filling out under the bright headlights of his whip as he moved forward. It was Drennen. He strolled toward him as if he didn't have a care in the world, and he didn't. Head tilted slightly to the side, his walk mirroring Denzel's as he took a quick scan of his surrounds. When Kreon's eyes locked onto his right hand, he noticed that it was black leather gloved and clutching tightly to The Ghost Gun.

"Pop the trunk." Drennen nodded to the rear of the car, wearing a no-nonsense expression plastered across his face. Kreon did as he said and stepped aside, leaving a clear path to the trunk of his car. He watched his dearest friend take another quick scan of his surroundings before slowly lifting the trunk. Not wanting to see what was about to happen next, Kreon turned his back to the trunk of his ride.

"Damn, Blood, we're here already? That was fa..." Jaekwon's words were cut short by automatic handgun fire, bullets coming back to back.

Poc! Poc! Poc! Poc! Poc!

Kreon's eyes pooled with tears and they came running down his cheeks. Although he hated his cousin for being a rat, he still had love for him. They'd grown up together, shared the same clothes, shoes, and had even eaten noodles off the same fork. Needless to say, he was in his feelings about having to let take place what he felt needed to be done.

Suddenly, Kreon's eyebrows arched and his nose scrunched up. He then wiped the wetness from his eyes with the back of his fist. *Fuck am I crying over this bitch ass nigga for? Family or no family, this nigga ratted on Unc and a gang of other niggaz. He got what the fuck he deserved.*

"Cheese eatin' mothafucka," Drennen scowled and spat on the corpse he'd created. He then tucked his burner on his waistline and slammed the trunk shut. Turning around to his right-hand man, he found him with his back to him. When he called out to him, he turned around with glassy eyes. He paid this no mind, as he tossed him the keys to his rental. Catching them, Kreon looked to his palm frowning and wondering what the fuck was up. "Take my car; I'll get rid of this piece of shit and pick it back up in the morning."

"Yep." Kreon threw his hood over his head and trekked back to the Nissan. He'd just pulled the driver side door open, when his nigga called him back. He turned toward him and threw his head back a little, like *What's up?*

"You did the right thang, homeboy," Drennen assured him. "This whole shit was a means to an end."

Kreon jumped behind the wheel of the Nissan, resurrected it, and pulled off.

*** *** ***

Omar drove up inside of the warehouse and murdered the engine of his big body Excursion. He threw opened the door and jumped down onto the graveled ground. He pulled a Newport cigarette from out of the pack of smokes that he was holding in his meaty hand and paced it between his thick lips. He pulled out a book of matches and stuck a flame off the black strip at the back of the book of matches. He was about to light his square when he saw something on the front of his shoe that made his brows furrow. Seeing it, he fanned out the match and tossed it aside. Taking the cigarette from out of his mouth, he bent down to take a closer look at his alligator skinned shoes with the buckle on the side.

"Aaah, fuck." He licked his thumb and tried to rub out the scratches at the front of his shoes, but they refused to come off. This was because the scratches were permanent. "Fuck, man. These are a three-hundred-dollar pair of fuckin' shoes." He stuck the square behind his ear and stuck the pack of smokes inside of the top pocket of his shirt. He licked his thumb once again and tried to rub the scratches out, but they stayed put.

Though you may not drive a great big Cadillac
Gangsta whitewalls, tv antennas in the back
You may not have a car at all
But, remember brothers and sisters
You can still stand tall

Hearing Curtis Mayfield's *Diamond in the back* heading in his direction, Omar looked up ahead just in time to be blinded by bright florescent orbs that illuminated him, causing his face to ball up. He threw his hand above his brows. He then narrowed his eyelids and stared ahead, seeing that it was the man that he'd came to see. He was behind the wheel of a beautiful '76 Fleetwood Cadillac with all of the trimmings. It was Easter bunny white and matching leather seats. Its owner called the gorgeous vehicle Heaven. If Omar didn't know any better, he'd sworn his connect had brought the Caddy that very day, but that couldn't be any further from the truth.

The Cadillac stopped a few feet away from Omar. He could see his connect in the driver seat. His eyelids were shut and he was nodding his head, snapping both of his fingers. The man seemed to really be in the groove of the music. Suddenly, the man's movements slowed and he placed his hand on the steering wheel, tapping the ring he wore on his finger against it, rhythm in sync with the tune coming from his crystal-clear speaker system. The gold ring on his finger had an upside-down pyramid. Once the song finally ended and the man killed the engine of his enormous vehicle, he hopped out of his car, box under his arm. He took a step back from his Cadillac, still holding the box under his arm. A smile spread across his lips as he looked at his vehicle like it was a beautiful woman he was proud to have on his arm. He then approached the car and rubbed on its hood lovingly, kissing it affectionately. Next, he strolled off in Omar's direction. Without looking over his shoulders, he held up the remote control to his car and pressed the button on it, locking up his vehicle.

"Well, I won't botha askin' you if you in a good mood or not," Omar said, having observed the older man's dancing and smiling. As he neared him, he took in his appearance. He was a slender African-American man. He rocked a shiny bald head and a pencil thin goatee. At the moment, he was wearing a white v-neck and a black suit. On his feet was a pair of white, snakeskin wing-tipped cowboy boots.

"Man, I'm in a fucking great mood, and why wouldn't I be? I'm getting paid lovely doing what I do; I'm living like mothafucking big time movie stars and I'm fucking pretty, fine women every other night. Life is beautiful, truly, truly, beautiful."

"Aye, if you like it, then I love it, Roland." Omar cracked a smile.

"My man." Roland dapped him up and bumped fists with him.

"Now, let's get down to business. You took care of everything?" he inquired, rubbing his hands together in anticipation.

"Everything," Roland assured him, handing him the box. "You've gotta clean slate, my friend," he told him, watching him rummage through the contents of the box. There were several colorful disc cases containing CD's and DVD's with labels on them. The labels had J.E. and a number marked on them, as well as a time. This was the recorded evidence, as well as video footage of Khadafi's murder. "Every document and recording is in there." He stole a glance at what was inside of the box. Omar had just taken his hand out of the box, satisfied with the merchandise that he'd received.

"What about those two dicks?" Omar asked, sitting the box down at his feet and opening the back door of his Excursion. He took out a worn, brown leather bag and slammed the trunk shut.

"You're on your own when it comes to those cats, man." He raised his hands up like he didn't want any trouble. "If I was you though, I'd just try to stay off those dudes radar. I mean, it isn't like they have any evidence on you now. I made sure of that. Believe me, man, you don't wanna pop these studs. You don't even wanna began to think of the shit storm that would come behind the murders of two federal agents. Trust me. I'm one of them," he placed his hand to his chest.

Omar took a deep breath and said, "I Griff you. Here you go." He passed the leather bag to Roland and he unzipped it, peeked inside at all the money. Satisfied with what he'd seen, he zipped the bag back up and held it at his side. "You ain't gone count that?" He motioned to the bag of money.

"Nah," He made a face as he shook his head. "I'm a man with many connections. In the business that you're in, you need someone like me. I'm too valuable. You'd be a fool to fuck up this relationship of ours. You never know when you'll need me again."

Omar made a frowned up and nodded his head like, *this nigga got a point.* "You're a smart man."

"Thanks, black man. Until we meet again." He outstretched his hand and Omar gave him a firm handshake. As the older gentleman turned to walk away, he patted him on his back and proceeded back over to the box of evidence and drenched it in the lighter fluid that he'd placed inside of the glove box before he came to the meeting. He couldn't help hearing Roland's Cadillac roar back to life and Curtis Mayfield bleeding from its speakers.

Just be thankful for what you've got

Diamond in the back, sunroof top, diggin' the scene with a gangsta lean

When Omar looked in his direction, he saw him throw his hand up out of the window. He then returned the gesture and watched as he backed out of the warehouse, looking over his shoulder out of the back window of the enormous vehicle. Once Roland was out of sight, Omar took the time to light up a Newport, tossing the burning match on to the box. The cardboard box went up quickly in flames, its golden orange light illuminating his face. He watched the evidence burn for a time before hopping back behind the wheel of his Excursion and pulling off, red brake lights disappearing into the night.

CHAPTER EIGHT

Briiiiing! Briiiiing! Briiiiing!

"Mar Mar, answer the phone baby!" Odette called out from the bathroom, where she was perched on the toilet while reading a novel called *Mama* by Terry McMillan.

The telephone rang while Marquise was sitting in front of the television Indian style, playing his PlayStation 4. He looked back and forth between the tv and the telephone, which was on the kitchen wall. He was kicking ass in the game and didn't want to pause it. But, his mother calling out from the bathroom for him to answer it while she was relieving herself changed his mind altogether. Pressing pause, Marquise jumped to his feet in his Superman pajamas and jogged inside of the kitchen. Seeing the name on the caller I.D. caused a smile to stretch across his face. He hurriedly picked up the phone and brought it to his ear, barely capable of containing his excitement.

"Daddyyyyyyyy!" He cheerfully jumped up and down.

Odette froze stiff when she heard her son say, *Daddy.* Her eyes looked up from the book and stared off at nothing. It appeared as if she was under hypnosis, watching an object swing back and forth before her eyes. It was then that her mind brought her back to one of the many times he'd put his hands on her over something minute.

Flashback

"Here you go." Odette sat a plate of food down before Carlos, as he stuffed a napkin inside of the collar of his shirt. He licked his chops as he grabbed a fork and knife. Before his eyes, there was a smothered pork chop, rice, candy yams, and collard greens, his favorite. "I'ma go hop in the shower." She wiped her hands off on the apron and took it off. Tossing it onto the back of the chair, she then headed for the bathroom.

Carlos cut a cube out of the pork chop and shut his eyelids, chewing on it. At first, there was a jovial expression on his face, but then that was quickly replaced by a sour look. Tilting his head down, he spat the chewed-up piece of meat into the plate.

"All that mothafucking salt, bitch tryna kill me. Know I got high blood pressure," he complained and scowled. He rose to his feet, snatching the napkin out of his collar and letting it fall to the floor. Right after, he was storming towards the bathroom, his large hairy fists clenched. Boom! He kicked that son of a bitch open and a fog greeted him. He heard the shower water spraying inside of the tub, pelting the tiled walls. The hot liquid fogged up the glass sliding doors of the shower.

Seeing his wife's silhouette behind the glass sliding doors, Carlos marched over and snatched it open. A startled Odette turned around, and he punched her square in the face. The impact deflected her head off the wall, leaving a smear of blood behind as she fell inside of the tub. Her eyes were rolled back to their whites. She laid there moaning, the shower nozzle water pelting her.

Carlos stared down at her like she was the one that was tripping. "Get cho ass up and make me something else to eat! Fuck is yo' problem? Making me that salty ass chop!" He slowly turned around but kept his eyes lingering on her. Next, he was walking out of the bathroom like he just didn't leave his wife sleeping inside of the tub.

Present

That was just one of the ass whippings that Odette had gotten being with Carlos for the past eight years. He went from slapping her, to punching her, to stomping her out like she had gotten caught stealing or some shit. It tripped Odette out how her man had transformed after they'd shared their vows. He went from treating her like she came from a royal bloodline, to handling her like she was a whore that came up short on his trap every night.

After she had Marquise, he really started dogging her ass out. She believed it was because she lost the tight body and perky tits she possessed before her pregnancy. He didn't miss a chance to tell her how fat and disgusting she looked and how no one was going to want her, should they ever divorce. This brought Odette's self-esteem down. She started dressing raggedy and not giving a fuck about what her hair looked like. She felt low, so low that she knowingly allowed Carlos to fuck around with other women on her. She accepted this behavior because she was afraid of losing him and being alone. The bitch ass nigga actually had her believing that she couldn't find anyone. That absolutely no one would love her like he did. It was because of this that she stuck it out with him, suffering mental and physical abuse from his black hearted ass.

But, everyone has their breaking point; the straw that broke the camel's back was when Marquise had caught him smacking the dog shit out her. The sight terrified the little boy and had him sleeping outside their bedroom door to make sure that she was okay. When this happened, she knew that she had to get away from him before he killed her and/or mentally scarred her baby boy for the rest of his life.

Odette set her book aside on the sink. She then wiped herself and flushed the toilet, taking the time to wash her hands. Having dried them off on a towel on the rack, she opened the door and headed down the hallway. The closer she drew, the louder and clearer her son's voice became.

"Yeah, I've been a good boy. Have you?"

"Hahahahaha, yes, lil' man, your papa has been good."

"Did you get to shoot a gun yet?"

"Yeah."

"Will you teach me how to shoot?"

"Soon as you get old enough, papa will take you somewhere so you can practice."

"Yesssssss!" he called out, holding up his fist and yanking it down to his side.

"Lil' man, where is yo' momma?"

Seeing his mother's shadow on the floor as she approached, Marquise turned around to see her wearing a serious expression on her face.

"Oh, here she is, daddy."

"Okay, put her on son. I love you."

"I love you, too." He passed the telephone upward to his mother and darted back inside of the living room where he sat down Indian-style and un-paused his game, continuing to play.

Odette held the telephone to her ear with her shoulder and examined her finger nails. "Yeah, Carlos?" She rolled her eyes and blew hard, annoyed by the nigga. Truthfully, he was the last person on earth that she wanted to hear from.

"How are you, beautiful?"

"You get the divorce papers that I sent?"

"Well, damn, that's how you come at a nigga?"

"Yup, I'm tired of you ducking and dodging them papers. Do me a favor, sign them and ship them back, so we can have this shit over with," she told him.

"I'ma come see you, ma; we needa talk."

She looked over her shoulder to see if her son was around, but he wasn't. She brought the receiver end of the phone to her lips and responded in a hushed tone. "Look, we don't have a mothafucking thing to talk about unless it's your son. You and I are through, homeboy. Comprendé, ese?"

"Bitch, you musta ate cho spinach this morning, 'cause you gotta be feeling realllll strong, the way you talking to me. You musta forgotten how I give it up."

"I ain't forgot nothing, you piece of shit! Those days of you going upside my head are gone. I'll shoot cho big ass, before I let that shit happen again."

"The day you point a gun at me is the day you…"

Click!

She disconnected the call and headed to her son's room. She found him there, playing with his Legos. She decided to help him build the castle that he had in mind, a smile plastered across her lips.

Meanwhile

Carlos sat low in his rental, which was a white on white Maybach 626. He was dressed in all white from head to toe, like he was going to P-Diddy's White Party. He was heavy on the icy platinum jewels. A white L.A. fitted cap sat cocked to the side on his crown and designer sunglasses covered his eyes. His head was on a swivel, as he gnawed on a toothpick and took in his surroundings. O.T. Genesis' *Cut It* pumped from his luxury vehicle's speakers vigorously, vibrating the big body car's side view mirrors as he pushed that bad boy through the streets.

Carlos was a hefty six foot seven, Dominican nigga with short curly hair and a goatee that aligned his jaw perfectly. He had a caramel hue and freckles. His big doughy eyes, wide nose, and full lips were the perfect marriage to his face. Every time he smiled, the street lights would deflect off his platinum grill and cast a rainbow. Although this nigga Carlos was dressed like he was about to shoot the music video for the first single on his rap album, he was actually in the Navy. Well, he'd gotten kicked out not too long ago. See, homeboy got caught running drugs back and forth through the states. When his commanding officer caught him, he didn't give him up to The Boys. Nah, instead, he made him drop fifty grand on him and concocted a plan for him to get a dishonorable discharge.

Carlos wasn't mad about getting thrown out of the Navy, though. No, he had more than enough money to live comfortably for a lifetime, as long as he'd been trafficking. Hell, all his commanding officer did was grant him an early retirement. So, now, he was going to spend the rest of his days spending, fucking bad bitches, and plotting on another come up.

Carlos looked to his left, seeing the residence that he was looking for. Immediately, he busted a U-turn in the middle of the street, nearly hitting an oncoming car that blew its horn at him. He threw his middle finger at the irate driver but kept his eyes focused on the road. He pulled right up to the house that he was looking for and murdered his engine. Grabbing a bouquet of some of the most beautiful long stemmed, sexy red roses that he'd ever seen in his entire life, he hopped out of the Maybach and slammed the door shut. Hunching down, he clenched his jaws so that he could get a good look at his platinum grill. That bitch was polished and shining like a mothafucka. Afterwards, he adjusted his white blazer and blew his hot breath on his huge pinky ring, fogging up the flawless diamond that it held. He then rubbed the diamond on his cocaine white shirt, stepping on the curb.

He pushed open the gate and walked into the yard. He licked his lips and continued to chew on his gum, advancing in the direction of the front door of the house. Clearing his throat, he lifted his jeweled fist and knocked on the door. Having taken in his surroundings, he focused his attention back on the front door; it was just now being pulled open. He found Odette there with a surprised look on her face when she saw him standing before her. The way the color drained from her face made him think that she'd seen a ghost, but that didn't stop him from smiling as hard as a bitch.

"Honey, I'm home!" With a jovial expression on his face, his eyelids narrowed; he smiled so hard. "Well, damn, you don't look too happy to see yo' man," he spoke seriously, pushing the flowers into her arms. He kissed her on the cheek and made his way inside, looking around. The door was shut behind him when he made eye contact with his son, Marquise, who was sitting on his knees watching cartoons. The boy's face broke out in a wide smile seeing his father.

"Daddyyyyy." He jumped to his socked feet and ran towards his old man's arms open for an embrace. Carlos scooped him up in his arms and hugged him tight, kissing the side of his head.

"How's my lil' man, huh? You been holdin' down the house since yo' poppito's been gone?"

"Yeahhh." He threw his fists up.

"Good. Thata boy." His forehead bunched up, seeing the crucifix around his son's neck. "Mommy got chu a lil' somethin' somethin', huh?"

"No, mommy's boyfriend. Kreon."

"Mommy's boyfriend, huh?" His scowling face snapped to Odette. She had just placed the roses inside of a glass vase of water. A frightened expression swept across her face, hearing her son's words and seeing her son's face.

Carlos sat Marquise down and told him to go into his bedroom and shut the door. He also promised him that he would be in there shortly to play video games with him. After telling the boy that he loved him, he kissed him on top of his head and patted his butt, sending him off. As soon as he heard the bedroom door shut, Carlos started in on Odette. By this time, she was wiping off the kitchen table, acting as if nothing had just occurred.

"Soooo, uhh, who the fuck is Kreon?" he asked, heatedly.

"Who and what Kreon is, is no business of yours." She set him straight. "We've been broken up two years now. I sent chu those divorce papers, how many times?"

"Fuck you mean? I told you that we were going to work things out."

"And I told you that I didn't want to," she spoke with her back to him, still wiping off the table. Odette had stopped fucking with Carlos when she found out that he was fucking with some girl off his base where he was stationed. The girl had gotten knocked up and, when he had denied her and her child, she sent Odette a detailed letter about the affair. The news broke her heart; she even thought about taking her own life. Odette had finally had enough of Carlos' shit and dumped his trifling ass. She had her attorney draw up the divorce papers and sent them up to him. He refused to sign them, stating that he was going to work things out for the good of his family. Odette wasn't trying to hear any of that shit, though. As far as she was concerned, she and Carlos were done. The idea of them staying a family died the moment he stuck his dick into another woman.

"Oh, so it's like that?"

"That's the way you made it, sir," she answered, sitting the salt and pepper shakers in their rightful places.

"You know what? If you don't want to fuck witta nigga, fuck it! That's cool. I'll just bust me anotha bitch, one that looks wayyyyy betta than you. I mean, shit, it ain't like that's gone be hard to do." This insult caused her to snap around, looking like a She Devil with hateful, hurtful look in her eyes. "What? You act like I'm frontin' or somethin'. You ain't that cute; all you had going for you when we met at Home Depot were big titties and a fat ass. Keepin' it real, shorty, mad niggaz made a pool on who could hit that, and guess who won it." He licked his lips, rubbing hands like he was the bald-headed owner of Cash Money records. The blow was below the belt and sent tears jetting down his wife's cheeks.

Odette sniffled and wiped her eyes with the back of her fist. She took a couple of deep breaths and swallowed the lump of hurt that had formed inside of her throat.

"Nice to know." She nodded. "Now, I've got something for you." She brushed passed him and headed to one of the drawers inside of the kitchen. Seeing her pull one of them open caused an alarm to blare inside of his head. His brows creased with a line and he went to draw the largest knife from out of the wooden block, when he saw her pull out a couple of documents and an ink pen. After pushing the drawer shut with her hip, she made her way over in Carlos' direction.

Stopping before him, she held out the items in her hands. The line in his forehead deepened and he looked to the documents. They were the divorce forms. "I want chu to sign these and then get the fuck outta my house. We'll discuss later the days you'll have Marquise and child support."

"I'm not signin' a damn thang," he gritted and harped up a glob of yellowish phlegm, spitting it in her face. She squeezed her eyelids shut, just as the nasty goo splattered against her face. It slid down and outlined the side of her nose.

Calmly, Odette sat the paperwork and ink pen down on the table. Next, she wiped her face off with the bottom inside of her shirt. Taking a deep breath, she spit in his face, twice. He frowned up further and further each time. He became so furious that he clenched his jaws tight, displaying the bone structure in his face. Balling his large fist, he cracked her ass dead in her mothafucking eye. The force behind the blow sent her little ass slamming against the table and flipping it over. She fell to the floor hard. Slowly, she scrambled to her feet, moaning as her eye was in the beginning stage of swelling shut. The evil giant stalked over and kicked her in her side, knocking the fucking wind out of her. She crashed to her side, doubling over and wincing. He grabbed her by the front of her shirt and punched her in the face hard as hell, three times more. Cuts opened on her face, due to all the rings on his fingers.

Carlos let a barely conscious Odette fall to the floor, then looked to his ring bearing fingers. They were stained with her blood. He took the time to lick the rings clean with his wet tongue. Letting his fist drop to his side, he observed his handiwork proudly, before hauling off and kicking her in the ribs again. Adjusting his cap and straightening out the wrinkles in his shirt, the evil giant went on about his business. He played video games with his son the entire time that Odette laid on the floor, barely conscious.

"Daddy, where's mommy?" Marquise asked, having just finished whipping his father's ass in Madden.

"Oh, she's in the front taking a nap son. Come on, run that back." He adjusted himself where he was sitting down on the floor, preparing for another round.

Once the game was finally over, it was night. Carlos tucked his son in bed and kissed his forehead, promising that they would hang out tomorrow. Shutting the door, he trekked across the living room. His mean mug met Odette's face. She was sitting at the kitchen table, holding a freezer bag of ice to her ruined eye. A butcher's knife dangled between her legs, a gleam swept up the length of the blade. The way she was glaring up at homeboy, you would have thought that she was about to slice and dice his big ass.

Carlos shot her a look like *bitch, I wish you would*, before continuing out of the door. Odette shot to her feet and ran to the door. She had begun locking it, when she heard knocks at the door. Her heart nearly leaped out of her fucking chest, having been startled. Her eyes bulged out of her sockets and she gasped, slowly stepping backwards. She held up her butcher's knife and was ready to cut Carlos' Spanish ass up if he came through that door. She was expecting him to start kicking at the lock of the door; she gripped her weapon tighter. That's when the knocking continued.

"Yooooo, O, open up, momma; it's Kreon, boo." Her man's voice resonated through the door. She sighed with relief and her shoulders dropped. Holding up her butcher's knife with both hands, she lowered her head and took a deep breath. Afterwards, she peeled her eyelids open and her head snapped up. She took the blade into her other hand and unlocked the door, letting her boo inside of her home.

As soon as he saw the damage to her face, he stopped and turned around. He waited for her to lock the door back and face him before he started in on her. "Fuck happened to yo' face?" He held her face up to him, tilting her chin upwards. His face tightened, seeing that his true love resembled a boxer on the receiving of an ass whooping.

"Car... Carlos." She winced from the pain in her face. "Mommy... Kreon!" Marquise called as he wandered out of his bedroom, twisting his knuckle at the corner of his eye. He was half asleep.

Odette turned her back to her son, covering her face with her hands. Seeing this, Kreon stood before her and spoke to the boy himself.

"'Sup, lil' homie, why don't chu go lay back down? Yo' mom will be there in a minute."

"Ooookay." He yawned and stretched. "I love you."

"I love you too, lil' nigga." He watched him disappear through his bedroom door and shut it behind him. Afterwards, he turned back around to Odette and demanded an answer from her.

"Now, who put they mothafuckin' hands on you, Odette?" Kreon's eyebrow arched and he folded his arms across his chest, awaiting her answer.

Odette looked away and took a deep breath. She then looked back to her man, afraid to give him Carlos' name for fear of what he may do to him.

"If I tell you, you gotta promise me that..."

He shook his head no and said, "Unh unh, I'm not promisin' you a damn thing, you gon' gemme this pussy's name and I'ma handle 'em."

She stared into his eyes and remembered how cold they were the last time she looked into them. There wasn't any doubt in her mind that he'd deliver on the threat he'd made, but she had to tell him. She was his woman, and her loyalty belonged to him and only him. On top of that, she swore to never lie to him or hurt him.

"It was Marquise's father," she revealed to him.

"And for what?"

She went on to tell him about the divorce papers and Carlos beating on her.

"Fuck that nigga think this is? Bitch ass nigga done touched mine; now, I'ma crush his ass!" Kreon pulled out his .38 and checked its chamber, making sure it was fully loaded. Once the inspection was done, he closed it and stuck in the front of his Dickies. When he looked up, Odette was standing in his path with her arms outstretched, blocking the door.

"Baby, no, just let it go please," she pleaded, a tear rolling down from the eye that wasn't swollen shut. Odette was truly scared of what would happen if he went out into the streets looking for Carlos. She was well aware that Kreon wouldn't hesitate to bust his pistol over her. There weren't any ifs, ands, or buts about it. That's just how the nigga was behind the people that he loved.

"Get outta my way, O; this nigga gotta answer for putting his hands on my queen."

"Bae, please, I'm scared; I don't want anything to happen to you."

"Ain't a goddamn thang gon' happen to me, you needa be worried 'bout cha punk ass husband," he swore, with a dead ass serious expression written across his face. "Cause once I catch up with homeboy, it's gone be a lotta slow singin' and flower bringin', straight up. Now, move!"

"No!" she shouted back, stretching her arms across the doorway and sliding her legs apart, blocking his exit.

"Move, O, 'fore I-"

"'Fore you what? Beat me like he did?" Her eye pooled with water, obscuring her vision. Her nostrils flared and her chest jumped up and down. She was frightened and worried. "Is that what chu gon' do, babe? Beat on me like he did. Go ahead, if it'll make you feel better. Use me as your punching bag." She crossed her hands behind her back and stuck out her chin, tilting it up and closing her eyelids.

"Go…" she sniffled, teardrops dripping from off her chin. "Go for what chu know, ain't like I'm not use to getting my fucking head boxed in anyway." Her body trembled and a fresh set of tears slicked her cheeks wet before meeting the carpet.

"I'd never lay my hands on you, O; a nigga love you too much." He pressed his hand against his chest. "You my mothafuckin' rib." He patted the left side of his ribcage. "But yo' man hurt something I love, something I love more than myself. For that, he's gotta pay with his life."

"You'd leave Marquise to be raised without his father?"

"He ain't no good for lil' dude no way."

"Still…" She blinked her good eye and swallowed her spit. "He is his father and maybe, one day, things between them will be better. I can't allow you to rob him of that chance ever happening."

Kreon exhaled and dropped his head, massaging the bridge of his nose. She slowly approached him, gently taking the .38 from the front of his Dickies and tucking it at the small of her back.

"Now." Odette spread her arms open, looking at him with great grief scrolled across her face. "Hold me." He embraced her, squeezing her tight and allowing her to melt like butter against him. Her eyes turned into slits as she bit down into the fabric of his Champion hoodie, sobbing her eyes out and staining it darker. Her releasing her emotions vibrated his chest. He closed his eyes and tears outlined his eyelids, wetting his lashes. He sniffed snot back so that his nose wouldn't drip. His baby was hurting. Therefore, he was hurting too. If there was some way that he could zap all her sorrows away and embody it for him to feel, he would. No questions asked. He'd just do it. That's how much he cared about her. He'd rather he felt her pain, just so he could see her happy during rainy days like these. Damn, if there was somehow or some way, he would do it at the drop of a hat. Until then, he would stand by her side. Be all that she needed him to be. Her friend, her man, her therapist, her shoulder to lean on at times like these, he would be her rock.

As soon as Odette was asleep, Kreon rolled out of bed and grabbed his .38. After grabbing the divorce papers from off the nightstand, he made his way out of the door. Kreon hit the streets on the prowl. He didn't know much about Carlos, besides he loved hard liquor, premium cigars, and fast women. You could find all these at The Bar Fly.

CHAPTER NINE

It was raining when Carlos came strolling his big ass out of The Bar Fly with two tipsy blondes. He was en route to the Maybach he'd rented when he stopped to open his umbrella. He had been having trouble getting the goddamn thing to operate inside of the bar, so he figured he'd give it another shot once he'd gotten outside.

"Ah, there this mothafucka go." Carlos cracked a toothy smile, boasting his shiny grill again. He'd just gotten the mechanism to work. His umbrella had opened to its full potential, providing shade from the rain. The giant took the time to adjust his jacket before motioning the scarcely dressed women underneath the protection of his umbrella. The blondes snuggled up on either side of him, placing a hand at his back and the other at his waistline. The rain fell from the right, pelting the umbrella and the lower halves of those that sought its shelter. Carlos and his fuck-buddies for that night moved through the parking lot towards his vehicle. They'd gotten halfway there when he pulled his keys from out of his pocket and held the small remote attached to it at his Benz. The luxury vehicle's headlights flashed and then there was the sound of the locks coming undone.

Carlos snickered and smiled wickedly, thinking of all the freaky shit he had in mind for the white girls once he got them back to his hotel suite. He had a camera on deck and sedatives to put their asses out, just in case they weren't with the freaky shit he wanted to do to them. The way he saw it, with the long tab they'd left him with at the bar, they owed him a happy ending, a very happy ending, as far as he was concerned.

Towering over the two women, Carlos looked down at their plentiful bosoms and licked his chops. Although he loved a woman with a big old ass, he greatly appreciated one with a nice rack. There was something about a pair of big succulent titties that made him want to be cradled and breast-fed like a newborn baby.

"Mmmmhmmm." He shook his head like it should have been a crime for the white girls to have such breasts. He then told them to go to the car, so he could get a good look at them. His tall ass wanted to picture the sexual shit in his mind that he was going to do to them. He didn't tell them the reason, though. Nah, he would keep that all to himself.

Carlos stood in the rain while biting down on his curled finger and smiling mischievously. He watched as the blondes advanced in the direction of his rental, feeling the raindrops pitter patting against his face and body. Water rolled around his face and dripped off his chin, splashing on the wet parking lot ground. Feeling someone at his back, the expression dropped from his face and he turned around.

It was there he found Kreon. His head was tilted down and he was glaring up at him, .38 pistol held at his side. He stood where he was, motionless. It didn't even look like he was breathing. Carlos could only see the lower half of him though. The upper half was masked by the darkness. It wasn't until the dark clouds grumbled and lightening occasionally struck that the night exploded with light. This was when he saw glimpses of Kreon's frowning face and twisted lips. To Carlos, the nigga looked like a mothafucking demon.

"What's up, puto?" The word rolled off Kreon's tongue like he was fluent in Spanish, but he only knew a few words of the shit.

"Who the fuck are you?" Carlos looked him up and down. His loud voice drew the attention of the blondes. As soon as they saw the ratchet in Kreon's hand, they took off running, high heel shoes clicking hard on the asphalt. Hearing their footfalls at his rear, Carlos glanced back at them but turned his attention back to Kreon.

"Odette's new boyfriend… Kreon. We haven't been formally introduced, *Carlos*." He glared at him even harder, squaring his jaws. A vein pulsated at his temple.

"Oooooh, my wife's new nigga, I should have known." He smiled once again, thinking about how he had whipped her mothafucking ass back at her house. There wasn't any second guessing it; homeboy was there to defend his lady's honor.

"I got some paperwork here I need you to sign, slim." Kreon pulled some folded documents from his back pocket and showed them to him.

Carlos frowned when he saw the paperwork. He didn't have to see what was written on them to know that they were Odette's divorce documents. The giant glared at Kreon and tightened his jaws so much that they throbbed.

"You tell that bitch I ain't signin' a mothafuckin' thang," he said threateningly, pointing his large crooked finger at him.

Kreon stuck the paperwork into his back pocket and flashed his banger. "Oh, yeah? Well, this says otherwise, homeboy."

Carlos took off running towards his car, trying to make it to the gun he kept underneath the driver seat. He nearly slipped and fell but kept on running towards his destination. He'd just gotten there when a gunshot rang out, echoing throughout the night. Kreon let one off in the air. This made his lady's husband stop cold in his tracks and lift his hands in the air. He cursed himself for leaving his gun behind in his whip. The nigga had initially thought that he would be patted down before he was allowed entry inside of the bar, but he was mistaken. Now, he was hoping that his mistake wouldn't cost him his life.

Kreon stepped behind Carlos and pressed that cold steel to the back of his onion. He then told him to open the driver side door. As soon as he did as he was instructed, Kreon busted him in the face with the butt of his pistol. The impact sent blood flying and brought his big ass down to his knees. Kreon grabbed him by the collar of his shirt and continued his merciless beating of him. He was gritting and hatred was dancing inside of his pupils.

"Big bitch ass nigga, you put cho hands on my Mocha? Huh, dick sucka?" The blue steel crashed into Carlos' skull until it was bloody. It looked like someone had dyed it like an Easter egg.

Crack! Wap! Wop!

Kreon began beating his victim across the face with the butt of his revolver, swelling his eyelid shut and opening gashes on his cheek. Specks of blood clung to his hand. Still holding Carlos about the collar of his shirt, Kreon flipped the stained pistol around in his palm and stuck it inside of Carlos' grill, causing him to gag on the end of it.

"Gaggghhh!"

"You put cho dick tuggers on my woman, mothafucka! Now, you get to meet the dark side, bitch!" Kreon had a dangerous look in his eyes as he licked his lips, cocking back the hammer of the lethal weapon with his thumb while wrapping his finger around its trigger. Carlos groaned in pain as he turned his head to avoid the blood splatter when he pulled the trigger.

"Bayyybyyy!" Kreon's head snapped up hearing the familiar voice bellow. He narrowed his eyelids, as the rain drops pelted his face and dripped off his eyebrows. His forehead wrinkled as he leaned forth and saw Odette running as fast as she could in his direction. She'd left her car's driver side door wide open. Little momma was dressed in a wife beater, basketball shorts, and mixed matched sneakers. He could tell by her attire, she'd hurriedly gotten dressed to come find him before he could send her husband to meet with the angels… or the demons.

Kreon peered closer and saw Marquise in the backseat window. His face and hands were pressed against the glass.

Every time he breathed, his nostrils would fog up the window. His eyes were wide and curious.

Odette stopped where she was, with her chest jumping up and down as she breathed heavily. Her eyelids were narrowed into slits as she stared at her soulmate while whipping her head from left to right, telling him no. The rain had left her face and her wife beater was partially wet. She didn't care though. All she wanted to do was save her man from breaking the sixth commandment: *Thou Shalt Not Kill.* "He... he isn't worth it, babe; forget him. He's a piece of shit and the biggest mistake in life that I've ever made. He and I are done. It's all about you and me now, Kre and O." Kreon looked from Carlos' wincing face to his lover, trying to make his decision. The G in him cried for blood, while the love of his lady called for forgiveness. "Please, bae, for me." She interlocked her fingers and held them up. Her eyes pleaded with him not to push that fuck nigga'z hairline back. His eyes darkened and his jaws locked so hard that they twitched.

"Grrrr." Kreon closed his eyelids and blew hot air from his nostrils and mouth. He shook his head. *What a sucka for love I am,* he thought. Right after, he was tucking his .38 on his waistline and throwing open the door of Carlos' ride, planting his punk ass into the driver seat. After shaking him to, he handed him an ink pen and smacked the divorce papers down against the horn. When the giant's eyes focused on the documents and he realized what it was, rage seized his eyes and he gritted. His wife-beating ass was as hot as a tea kettle.

"Fuck you!" he spat venom in his direction. "I ain't signin' sh..." When that shiny hard thang made an indention into his cheek, he shut the fuck up real quick. He knew that a banger was no joke and the nigga holding it wasn't either.

"You ain't signing what?" Kreon shot daggers at him with clenched jaws, trigger finger itching. Carlos' eyes shot to the pistol, then back up into its welder's eyes. Defiance debuted inside of his pupils and his lips moved like he was about to say something smart. "I dare you, I double fucking dare you, mothafucka." He licked his lips and prayed for his boo's spouse to get smart, so that he could put his brains on the dashboard.

"Babe." Odette grasped his arm, trying to calm the beast that was inside of him, rattling its cage and begging to be set free to tear some shit up. He was like The Hulk and she was Betty. It was something about her presence that settled him a little, but it didn't quite offset the course of his gangsta all the way. It would always be there, lying in the cut hidden, ready, and waiting.

"If you know like I know, you'd get to jotting," he swore with danger flickering in his eyes. "Cause this is a G, you don't wanna test, homie." He smacked his meaty hand up against his chest. "Trust and believe."

Carlos' eyes darted to Odette for reassurance that homeboy with that .38 to his cheek would really make him part with his life. She gave him a nod, and that's all he needed to know to confirm that old boy was with the shit. He pressed the metal button at the butt of the pen and jotted down his John Hancock on the sheets of paper. Angrily, he swung the papers around, holding them out towards Odette.

"Gone take it, baby," Kreon told his woman, keeping his evil eyes on bitch-boy, in case he wanted to buck.

Odette looked at the signatures of the divorce papers over, folded them up, and stuck them inside of her basketball shorts. "We straight, boo?"

"Yeah, we're straight," Kreon replied, still focused on Carlos. "You can take it home now."

"Kreon, don't-"

"Don't worry, I'm not gone kill his punk ass. I should though."

"Okay." She took a deep breath and exhausted hot air, slumping her shoulders. With that, she trekked back to her whip and drove off, leaving her boyfriend and her husband alone.

"I want you to listen and listen good," Kreon began. "I want you to stay the fuck away from O. Don't you dare call, text, tweet, DM, or even fucking write her. 'Cause if I catch wind of it, I'm coming back for you and I'ma leave yo' punk ass wherever the fuck I find you. You got that?" There was a long silence, as the two men mad dogged one another. "I'm not in the habit of repeating myself."

"Got it," Carlos responded like it was killing him to do so and, truthfully, it was. He wasn't used to having another man check his ass on shit. You see, even in the army, he was an authority figure.

"Good." *Wappp!* Kreon cracked him upside the head with the butt of that blue steel and he grabbed the side of his bleeding head, squeezing his left eyelid shut so blood wouldn't get into it.

"Gaaah, fuck!" Carlos gritted, slowly getting out of the car in time to see Kreon cranking up his Pontiac and pulling off. He chased after the car while holding his oozing head, hurling insults and threats. "You're dead, you hear me, asshole? You are so fucking dead!" He jabbed the air with a crooked finger, as spittle flew from off his lips. When he got tired of chasing behind the Pontiac, he stood in the middle of the street, watching its back lights.

"This is far from over, bitch!" he spat on the ground and continued to watch the back of Kreon's ride, until it had disappeared into the night.

***

Royce sat between the legs of a thick redbone, getting his shoulder-length hair braided. His head slightly shook as she handled the task at hand, while he twisted up a blunt for them to indulge in. Royce was a tall, dark caramel nigga with hazel eyes and bushy chin hair. He was skinny and had tattoos that covered him from neck to sleeves. Burgundy Dickies hung off his bony ass and corduroy house shoes were on his feet. His eyes were looking up at the television screen as he licked the blunt closed, watching an episode of Empire. Taking the blunt into one hand, he held the flame of his Bic lighter to it until its tip was ember. Next, he took a couple of puffs and passed it up over his head to homegirl. She took it and had her way with it before passing it back to him. Royce narrowed his eyelids into slits as smoke wafted into his face from him sucking on the end of his blunt.

Knock! Knock! Knock!

"Fuck is it?" Royce hollered out.

Knock! Knock! Knock!

Royce stopped old girl from braiding his hair and grabbed his Desert Eagle off the coffee table. After cocking the slide on it, he hopped up from off the floor and advanced on the door. He peered through the curtains and saw who it was on the porch. Sighing with relief, he tucked that thang in the front of his pants and unchained and unlocked the door. As soon as he pulled the door open, he saw a very fucked-up Carlos. He was holding an ice pack to the side of his face. His left eye was swollen shut and his face was wide on one side and bloody. The collar of his shirt was stained pink, thanks to the blood that had slicked down his neck.

"Blood, who in the fuck beat cho ass?" Royce looked him up and down, having shut the door behind him. He couldn't believe what the fuck had happened to him.

"I got jumped, man." Carlos looked at the ice pack and then put it back to the side of his face. His shit was hurting bad as a mothafucka, but not more than his ego. When Kreon had given him that work, his gangsta shrunk in size.

"Jumped?" His forehead deepened with lines. "Fuck jumped yo' big ass, nigga? And for what?"

"Some lil' niggaz, man, took my money, my jewels, and credit cards; the whole nine yards." Carlos paced the floor. He had taken off all his jewelry and cash and stashed it inside of his safe at his house. He did this so that his story would be more believable. See, his cousin Royce was a straight up mothafucking goon; he didn't have any problems with letting that choppa go off. Carlos wanted him with him when he went on his mission to lay that nigga, Kreon, down. He knew that his relative was official tissue and would be down to roll with him, but not if he found out that it was just one nigga that had launched the brutal assault against him.

"Awww, fuck naw, Blood!" Royce snarled and looked to his bitch. "Tela, go get my shit out the closet." The redbone girl hopped up and went to retrieve her man's gun. "You know where these fools at?"

"One of them stays by my wife's way," he told him straight up, looking him dead in his eyes.

"Odette?" Royce's forehead crinkled.

"Yeah." He slightly nodded.

"Babe," a voice came from their rear. When they looked, the redbone chick was there with an AK-47. He took the assault rifle from her and checked its banana clip before injecting it back in, cocking its hammer.

Click! Clack!

"Hold this shit." He passed it off to Carlos while he got dressed. He threw some Nike baseball gloves and a hoodie on, making sure a wave cap was firm around his head. After wrapping the choppa up in a blanket, he tapped his cousin and they headed out of the house.

***

Odette had gotten home about 30 minutes ago from the incident down at The Bar Fly between her, Kreon, and Carlos. She didn't waste any time putting Marquise to bed and hopping on the telephone to tell her sister what happened. Now, she was pacing the floor frantically while cradling her telephone to her ear. Every five minutes, she found herself peeking through the blinds to see if Kreon had made it to her house. She was terribly worried that he may have gotten caught up with the police for pistol whipping her son's father. If he did, she was ready to rustle up the few dollars that she'd saved and pawn all her jewelry, including her wedding ring, to get him out if she had to. He was her man and she would do any and everything in her power for him. That's just how little momma was, ride or die.

"For real?" Shonda asked. She couldn't believe what her sister had just told her.

"Yeah."

"Gon', brotha in law, 'cause God knows that nigga Carlos needed a good ass whopping."

"I agree. But, now I'm worried that something has happened to him."

"You think the police may have snatched him up?"

"Yes. And there's no telling how that will go."

"You don't think he's fool enough to shoot it out with the police, do you?"

Now, Shonda was sounding worried about Kreon's safety. "Kreon's unpredictable, there's no telling, especially with his condition."

"Condition?"

"His mental illness." She peered out between the blinds.

"Mental illness? Wait a minute. You mean to tell me that..."

"Love you, gotta go." She disconnected the call and hurriedly unlocked the door.

***

Kreon pulled up four cars down from Odette's house and hopped out of the Nissan. He walked down the sidewalk, looking at the dry blood that covered his hands and the sleeves of his hoodie. As soon as he got into Odette's house, he was going to wash up and have her stash his pistol. Although his boo claimed her man was a street nigga, he wasn't taking any chances on him, abiding by the unwritten codes of the streets. For all he knew, the police were combing the streets looking for him at that very moment.

Kreon's cellular was inside of his pocket and set on silent, so he didn't know Odette had been blowing him up and trying to find out exactly where he was. He had programmed his cell this way, so he wouldn't hear her calling him on his way to handle her husband. The last thing he needed was his cell ringing, disturbing his thinking. See, he needed to conclude exactly what he was going to do. He had it in mind to get him to sign the divorce papers and slump his ass, or just slump his ass. That's when he thought about what Odette said back at her house, about not wanting Marquise to grow up without his father. Kreon knew the struggle growing up without his father, too well. He didn't meet the man he was told was his father until he was ten years old. He was around until he was fifteen, and those five years were the worse of his life, hands down.

It was because of this reason and this reason only, that he allowed that punk ass nigga, Carlos, to keep his life. If it hadn't been for little Marquise, he would have peeled that nigga'z cap back.

Kreon was so caught up in the examining of his bloodstained hands, he was ignorant to the presence of danger. An Envoy truck with it headlights out was creeping up the street. From the movements of the silhouettes inside, you could tell that they were retrieving their weapons and making sure that they were locked and fully loaded. The back-passenger side window descended and a large man appeared in it.

"Slow up, slow up!" Carlos said to Royce, from the front passenger seat of the Envoy truck. He'd just spotted Kreon walking up the block, en route to Odette's house. The hulk of a man scowled and smiled behind the bandana he was wearing on the lower half of his face and gripped his AK-47 in his hands firmly.

"That's him?" Royce asked, wanting to be sure.

"Yeah, that's that mothafucka." He nodded, eyes stuck on his mortal enemy.

"Alright." He flicked the roach end of a blunt out of the window, sending embers flying. He then pulled his red bandana up over the lower half of his face, sitting his Desert Eagle in his lap. He murdered the headlights of the truck and brought that bitch to a crawl up the block. The SUV blended into the night, making it hard to see to the naked eye.

Carlos let his window down and the night's cool air rushed inside, ruffling his clothing. He could hear his heart pounding inside of his chest, as well as inside of his ears. The moment of truth was near. He had to deliver on his threat to Kreon and show his cousin that he was about that life, just like he was. The closer he drew to Kreon, the more two sounds grew to him. That was his breathing and the beating of his heart, his adrenaline rushing the blood through his veins. Slowly, he inched himself out of the window and made to take aim at the nigga he planned on smoking. As soon as he met the surprised look on his face, he was pointing the dangerous end of his AK at him.

"Mothafucka, you and yo' homies jumped my relative and you thought chu were gonna get away with it?" Royce talked that shit behind his bandana. His eyes were threatening and his body language displayed hostility. Hearing this chilling voice, Kreon whipped his head around.

"Yeah, nigga, pop that shit now!" Carlos' menacing eyes bore into his enemy's and his finger curled around the trigger.

Kreon's eyelids snapped open and he gasped.

Odette came running outside to the front porch; hands to her face, she screamed, "Krrrreeeeeoooooon!"

Fuck, niggaz caught me out here slippin', Kreon thought to himself, seeing the barrel of Carlos' assault rifle spitting flames.

***

Newport wedged between her fingers, Ella zipped up the last of her duffle bags and dropped it on the floor beside the other duffle bag. Stepping before the mirror of the dresser, she took one last pull from her square and sat it down in the ashtray. Smoke wafted from it and disappeared in the air. Picking up a beige rubber band, she stared at her reflection and pulled her graying hair back into a ponytail, tangling the rubber band around it. Her eyelids had swollen from crying for so long, and her eyes were pink and glassy. Her cheeks were slicked wet, having shed her so many tears.

Ella couldn't believe her son blamed her for his mental illness. She couldn't see how she was solely responsible for his condition. Sure, she housed the man that harassed and abused him, but there were other incidents that contributed to him being emotionally disturbed. She refused to hold all the weight herself. Sure, she wasn't the ideal parent, but who was? Ella did the best she could raising her son. She did everything in her power to give him a better life than she had. So, even if she failed, she could sleep at night knowing that she tried.

Ella took another pull from the end of her cancer stick, pulling smoke into her lungs. Allowing the intoxicating fog to roll around inside of her chest, she blew it back out with the other smoke lingering around her. Afterwards, she mashed the cigarette out inside of the ashtray, leaving a black smear behind. Next, she threw on her corduroy jacket with the wool around the collar and jotted down something on a slip of paper. She folded the paper up and stuck it inside of an envelope, licking it closed. Having signed her son's name on the front of the envelope, she grabbed her duffle bags and headed for the living room. Coming across the portrait of herself and a younger Kreon, she stopped where she was and turned around. Dropping her duffle bags on the floor, she picked up the portrait and admired it. A smile etched across her face.

"My baby boy, my sweet, sweet baby boy," She kissed her hands and placed it to the glass of the portrait, sliding her fingers down the center of it. Next, she tucked it inside of her jacket, grabbed her duffle bags, and headed out of the door. Holding the door open, she took one last look at the apartment before taking her leave.

***

Drennen was gangsta leaning in Kreon's Pontiac, gripping the steering wheel with one hand. He nodded his head while listening to George Clinton's *Atomic Dog*, spitting the lyrics along with him. If any of the cars in the lanes beside him knew his current situation, they'd think he'd lost his mothafucking mind. And who could blame them? He was cruising through the streets without a care in the world with a dead body in his trunk.

Sometime later, Drennen's forehead creased with lines. This was because he saw orange cones in the street that was leading traffic to one side of the road, as well as a lit-up sign that read, *check point ahead.* Drennen's heart quickened in his chest. It was at this time that he thought about Jaekwon's body in the trunk and the gun that he'd used to kill him, which was underneath his seat. Before he knew it, he was being forced to drive in one lane by cones. The palms of his hands had grown moist, idling in the lane and seeing that there were only three vehicles ahead of him. Drennen believed that he was fucked with a capital F. The police usually asked for your driver's license and checked to see if you were under the influence. He didn't drink or smoke, so he was good as far as being under the influence, but he didn't have any L's. Hell, he had been locked up for the past few years, so it wasn't any way that he could provide proof of that.

Fuck that. I'ma hold court in these streets before I go back to the pen. He removed The Ghost Gun from underneath his seat, tucking it in between the seat and console. As soon as the cop asked for his driver's license, he was going to blow his wig back. Drennen pulled to a stop and a burly officer with a bushy mustache approached his window, knocking on it. Smiling, the ex-con let the window down and greeted the law enforcer.

"Hey, how are you doing there, partner? May I see your license and registration please."

"Sure. I got it right here, sir." Drennen smiled at the officer. Turning his head away from him, he scowled and went to pull his weapon.

***

Po sat on the bench, leaning forward with his hands clasped. His head was tilted upwards and his eyes were taking in everyone that was inside of the holding cell with him. He wasn't tripping off any of the niggaz there, because he and his crew outnumbered them. Po and his niggaz had been there nearly a week; today, the bus was coming to take them up to the County jail. He had been calling his older brother, Kennan's, house since the day before, but he'd yet to get an answer. Po figured he'd try calling again today, in hopes that someone would answer.

There was laughter and talking amongst the men inside of the holding cell. Po's niggaz chopped it up amongst themselves about the time they were looking at for the guns and drugs they were caught with, while Po sat at the end of the bench lost in thoughts of his own. Out of all his people, Po was the one looking at never seeing the sunlight again, being that he was already a two-time loser.

With this case, he was looking at twenty-five years to life under California's three strike law. If nothing short of a miracle happened, he knew that he was washed up, but he wasn't just going to lie down without getting some get-back. Fuck that. He wouldn't be able to sleep at night knowing that the bitch responsible for him being locked up for an eternity was still out in the free world.

Seeing one of the fools inside of the cell had just gotten off the phone, Po jumped to his feet and strolled over to it casually.

Picking up the telephone, Po placed a collect call to his brother again. He cracked a slight grin when he heard someone answer the telephone. It was a woman. His exchange with her was brief. Afterwards, she handed her husband the telephone.

"Bruh bruh, it's me, Po."

"Sup, lil' nigga? Fuck you doin' locked up?" He took the time to take a pull from whatever he was smoking and blew out smoke into the air.

Po told Kennan exactly how he'd gotten locked up. He then went on to tell him in code what he wanted done about it.

"Yeah, my nigga, if this shit goes left, I'm not neva gone see a sunset again."

"Keep yo' head up loved one. Yo' blood got chu faded."

"True that. Peace." Po disconnected the call and shuffled back over to the bench. Once he got to the space that he was sitting, he found a young nigga there that looked like he was with the shit. The fool had tattoos on his face that made little to no sense and dreadlocks that hung over his eyes. His menacing eyes peered up at Po, but he wasn't pumping fear into his heart. Nah, that nigga Po was far from pussy. He was cut from a cloth that wasn't even made anymore.

Po's eyebrows arched and his nose scrunched up. He balled his hands into fists at his sides, making the old scars and missing knuckles there more prominent.

"Fuck up off of my spot, nigga!" he ordered with authority in his voice.

"Fuck you think you talking to?" Dreadlocks jumped to his feet, hair bouncing on his shoulders.

"You, pussy!" he spat the word *pussy* with emphasis, raining spittle in homeboy's face.

"Nigga, you got me fucked…" Dreadlocks went to fire on Po and all his niggaz surrounded him. Their hard faces and twisted lips dared him to make a move so that they could use his dreadlocks to mop up his own blood. Dreadlocks took a look around at all the threatening faces encircling him and knew instantly that he didn't stand a chance.

"This not what chu want, homie. Now, get the fuck…" Po kicked dreadlocks so hard in his ass; he fell to the cold, filthy floor. Him and his crew watched him scramble to his feet and retreat to the corner, holding his buttocks and looking over his shoulder to make sure that they weren't about to jump his ass.

"Punk ass nigga!"

"Bitch ass mothafucka!"

"Fuck-nigga!"

These were just some of the words uttered by Po and his niggaz. One of them asked could they pound dreadlocks out, but he told them to chill. Afterwards, on his orders, they disassembled and left him by his lonesome. Po pulled up his jeans and sat down on the bench, leaning forward and clasping his hands together. Deep in his thoughts, he stared at the ground and a wicked smile suddenly etched across his face. He started off giggling, then chuckling, and, finally, full out laughing his ass off. The nigga laughed so hard that tears came running out of the corners of his eyes. He had his head tilted back and his hand on his stomach, cracking the fuck up.

What was so funny you ask? Well, Po's brother, Kennan, was said to be one of the most feared men in Southern California. You couldn't help mentioning murder and his name in the same breath. He was known for gunplay. The mothafucka had a reputation that stretched longer than Crenshaw Blvd. Unleashing him was the equivalent of letting a lion loose in civilization. This was because there was sure to be chaos and pandemonium. Po was laughing because Ella didn't know the trouble that was headed her way, and she'd be surprised when old Kennan showed up on her doorstep.

"Hahahahahahahahahaha."

Po doubled over laughing, holding his stomach with both hands. His crew and the rest of the niggaz in the cell were standing around, staring at him like he'd lost his fucking mind.

"Hahahahahahahahahaha."

"Man, they locked us up with a real mothafuckin' loon," one of the detainees said in a hushed tone to one of the men standing near him, keeping his eyes on Po.

"Hahahahahahahahahaha."

"You ain't neva lied," the man replied, keeping his eyes on a laughing Po as well.

"Hahahahahahahahahaha."

To Be Continued...
God Bless the Trappers
Coming Soon

Submission Guideline

Submit the first three chapters of your completed manuscript to ldpsubmissions@gmail.com, subject line: Your book's title. The manuscript must be in a .doc file and sent as an attachment. Document should be in Times New Roman, double spaced and in size 12 font. Also, provide your synopsis and full contact information. If sending multiple submissions, they must each be in a separate email.

Have a story but no way to send it electronically? You can still submit to LDP/Ca$h Presents. Send in the first three chapters, written or typed, of your completed manuscript to:

LDP: Submissions Dept
Po Box 870494
Mesquite, Tx 75187

DO NOT send original manuscript. Must be a duplicate.

Provide your synopsis and a cover letter containing your full contact information.

Thanks for considering LDP and Ca$h Presents.

BOW DOWN TO MY GANGSTA

By **Ca$h**

TORN BETWEEN TWO

By **Coffee**

BLOOD STAINS OF A SHOTTA **III**

By **Jamaica**

STEADY MOBBIN **III**

By **Marcellus Allen**

BLOOD OF A BOSS **V**

By **Askari**

LOYAL TO THE GAME **IV**

LIFE OF SIN

By **T.J. & Jelissa**

A DOPEBOY'S PRAYER **II**

By **Eddie "Wolf" Lee**

IF LOVING YOU IS WRONG… **III**

LOVE ME EVEN WHEN IT HURTS **II**

By **Jelissa**

TRUE SAVAGE **VI**

By **Chris Green**

BLAST FOR ME **III**

A BRONX TALE

By **Ghost**

ADDICTIED TO THE DRAMA **III**

By **Jamila Mathis**

LIPSTICK KILLAH **III**

CRIME OF PASSION **II**

By **Mimi**

WHAT BAD BITCHES DO **III**

KILL ZONE **II**

By **Aryanna**

THE COST OF LOYALTY **II**

By **Kweli**

SHE FELL IN LOVE WITH A REAL ONE **II**

By **Tamara Butler**

LOVE SHOULDN'T HURT **III**

RENEGADE BOYS **II**

By **Meesha**

CORRUPTED BY A GANGSTA **IV**

By **Destiny Skai**

A GANGSTER'S CODE **III**

By **J-Blunt**

KING OF NEW YORK III

By **T.J. Edwards**

CUM FOR ME **IV**

By **Ca$h & Company**

GORILLAS IN THE BAY

De'Kari

THE STREETS ARE CALLING

Duquie Wilson

KINGPIN KILLAZ II

Hood Rich

STEADY MOBBIN' **III**

Marcellus Allen

SINS OF A HUSTLA II

ASAD

HER MAN, MINE'S TOO **II**

Nicole Goosby

GORILLAZ IN THE BAY **II**

DE'KARI

TRIGGADALE II

Elijah R. Freeman

THE STREETS ARE CALLING **II**

Duquie Wilson

<u>Available Now</u>

<u>RESTRAINING ORDER</u> **I & II**

By **CA$H & Coffee**

<u>LOVE KNOWS NO BOUNDARIES</u> **I II & III**

By **Coffee**

<u>RAISED AS A GOON I, II, III & IV</u>

<u>BRED BY THE SLUMS I, II, III</u>

<u>BLAST FOR ME I & II</u>

<u>ROTTEN TO THE CORE I III</u>

By **Ghost**

<u>LAY IT DOWN</u> **I & II**

<u>LAST OF A DYING BREED</u>

<u>BLOOD STAINS OF A SHOTTA I & II</u>

By **Jamaica**

<u>LOYAL TO THE GAME</u>

<u>LOYAL TO THE GAME II</u>

<u>LOYAL TO THE GAME III</u>

By **TJ & Jelissa**

<u>BLOODY COMMAS I & II</u>

SKI MASK CARTEL I II & III

KING OF NEW YORK I II

By **T.J. Edwards**

IF LOVING HIM IS WRONG…I & II

LOVE ME EVEN WHEN IT HURTS

By **Jelissa**

WHEN THE STREETS CLAP BACK I & II III

By **Jibril Williams**

A DISTINGUISHED THUG STOLE MY HEART I II & III

LOVE SHOULDN'T HURT I II

RENEGADE BOYS

By **Meesha**

A GANGSTER'S CODE I & II

By **J-Blunt**

PUSH IT TO THE LIMIT

By **Bre' Hayes**

BLOOD OF A BOSS **I, II, III & IV**

By **Askari**

THE STREETS BLEED MURDER **I, II & III**

THE HEART OF A GANGSTA I II& III

By **Jerry Jackson**

CUM FOR ME

CUM FOR ME 2

CUM FOR ME 3

An **LDP Erotica Collaboration**

BRIDE OF A HUSTLA **I II & II**

THE FETTI GIRLS **I, II& III**

CORRUPTED BY A GANGSTA I, II & III

By **Destiny Skai**

WHEN A GOOD GIRL GOES BAD

By **Adrienne**

A GANGSTER'S REVENGE **I II III & IV**

THE BOSS MAN'S DAUGHTERS

THE BOSS MAN'S DAUGHTERS II

THE BOSSMAN'S DAUGHTERS III

THE BOSSMAN'S DAUGHTERS IV

THE BOSS MAN'S DAUGHTERS **V**

A SAVAGE LOVE **I & II**

BAE BELONGS TO ME

A HUSTLER'S DECEIT I, II

WHAT BAD BITCHES DO I, II

By **Aryanna**

A KINGPIN'S AMBITON

A KINGPIN'S AMBITION **II**

I MURDER FOR THE DOUGH

By **Ambitious**

TRUE SAVAGE

TRUE SAVAGE II

TRUE SAVAGE **III**

TRUE SAVAGE **IV**

TRUE SAVAGE **V**

By **Chris Green**

A DOPEBOY'S PRAYER

By **Eddie "Wolf" Lee**

THE KING CARTEL **I, II & III**

By **Frank Gresham**

THESE NIGGAS AIN'T LOYAL **I, II & III**

By **Nikki Tee**

GANGSTA SHYT **I II &III**

By **CATO**

THE ULTIMATE BETRAYAL

By **Phoenix**

BOSS'N UP **I , II & III**

By **Royal Nicole**

I LOVE YOU TO DEATH

By Destiny J

I RIDE FOR MY HITTA

I STILL RIDE FOR MY HITTA

By **Misty Holt**

LOVE & CHASIN' PAPER

By **Qay Crockett**

TO DIE IN VAIN

By **ASAD**

BROOKLYN HUSTLAZ

By **Boogsy Morina**

BROOKLYN ON LOCK I & II

By **Sonovia**

GANGSTA CITY

By **Teddy Duke**

A DRUG KING AND HIS DIAMOND I & II III

A DOPEMAN'S RICHES

HER MAN, MINE'S TOO

By Nicole Goosby

TRAPHOUSE KING **I II & III**

KINGPIN KILLAZ

By **Hood Rich**

LIPSTICK KILLAH **I, II**

CRIME OF PASSION

By **Mimi**

STEADY MOBBN' **I, II**

By **Marcellus Allen**

WHO SHOT YA **I, II**

Renta

GORILLAZ IN THE BAY

DE'KARI

TRIGGADALE

Elijah R. Freeman

GOD BLESS THE TRAPPERS I, II, III

THESE SCANDALOUS STREETS I, II, III

FEAR MY GANGSTA I, II

THESE STREETS DON'T LOVE NOBODY I, II

Tranay Adams

THE STREETS ARE CALLING

Duquie Wilson

SINS OF A HUSTLA

ASAD

BOOKS BY LDP'S CEO, CA$H

TRUST IN NO MAN

TRUST IN NO MAN 2

TRUST IN NO MAN 3

BONDED BY BLOOD

SHORTY GOT A THUG

THUGS CRY

THUGS CRY 2

THUGS CRY 3

TRUST NO BITCH

TRUST NO BITCH 2

TRUST NO BITCH 3

TIL MY CASKET DROPS

RESTRAINING ORDER

RESTRAINING ORDER 2

IN LOVE WITH A CONVICT

Coming Soon

BONDED BY BLOOD 2

BOW DOWN TO MY GANGSTA

www.ingramcontent.com/pod-product-compliance
Lightning Source LLC
Chambersburg PA
CBHW070044260626
47159CB00005B/2116